Home to Hardscuffle and All That Jazz

Charles Howell

Cold Tree Press

Nashville, Tennessee

This book is a work of fiction. While as in all fiction, the literary perceptions and insights are based on experience, all names, characters, places, and incidents are either products of the author's imagination or are used fictitiously. No reference to any real person is intended or should be inferred.

Published by Cold Tree Press, Nashville, Tennessee

Library of Congress Number: 2007938825
Cover Photo:
Robert "Bob" Yellin

ISBN-13: 978-1-58385-193-7
ISBN-10: 1-58385-193-3

Introduction

This story is not about the Ku Klux Klan. It is about the people who were or easily could have been, ruined by the Klan. The story of the Indiana Klan is in the prologue and I invite you to learn about it there.

The seed of information that lead me to the Klan in Indiana was an experience by the family of my wife, Julie Harb Howell. Her mother and father were immigrants from Ramallah, Palestine. He came in 1919 as a teenager, albeit not a very big one. He stood less than 5 feet and weighed about 120 pounds. Ten years later, he arranged, through an Orthodox Priest, marriage to the prettiest girl in Ramallah! By this time, he could tell his friends in the old country that the streets of America were truly paved with gold. They married there and came to the new world to settle in Evansville, Indiana where he went into the import business with a cousin who soon took his disagreeable wife back home. Later the powerful Indiana Klan members in town frightened him because of his Semitic heritage. He moved his family to San Francisco, including a wife newly pregnant with a second child, where they lived above the grocery store of her parents. He hit the road going door to door again selling his imported merchandise and regularly visiting the local offices of Fenner and Bean, his stockbrokers.

The geography is familiar territory to me as are some of the characters. I was born on the corner of the original Hardscuffle Road (extended) and the Nashville to Franklin Turnpike. Many of the characters are from that era. Hardscuffle is the path that many of the former slaves and their offspring lived for almost a hundred years. Hardscuffle has now been gentrified and the name is no longer used. The tarpaper shacks and log cabins are gone and replaced by a hotel and lovely residences along the way.

Dedication

This book is dedicated to those who inspired it: to my in-laws Abrahim Shehadeh Harb and Bahia Badran Harb and to Aunt Sarah Gentry and Uncle Bob Daniel both residents of my Hardscuffle Road who meant a great deal to me and who shaped my life for the better.

Words of Appreciation

With appreciation to the staff of the Indiana Historical Society, Bobby Dawson at Cold Tree Press, and the ladies on the beach at Sanibel Island who witnessed the beginning of my journey in 1996, to the Library Staff at Sanibel and to the other occasional readers of early drafts for their thoughtful comments. Of course, I pay tribute to my lovely wife of 53 years who only lost her patience every now and then. She told me more than once I was not married to a word processor and to pay more attention to my husbandly and fatherly responsibilities. Having spent more than 10 years writing this story should be proof enough that I had time to live up to all my commitments along the way!

Prologue

From The Indianapolis Star
THE CHANGING FACE OF INDIANAPOLIS: 1920-1929
Ku Klux Klan Dominance Marked an Ugly Era for City
ROB SCHNEIDER
Published: Dec. 23, 1999

It was not too long ago that the Ku Klux Klan took to the Statehouse steps, fighting broke out and a handful of people were injured.

Some 35 Klansmen showed up for the rally. The crowd that turned out that October day in 1993 – which included hundreds of anti-Klan protesters – was estimated at more than 1,000.

If some people saw it as a throwback to long-ago times, they were wrong. If it had been, there wouldn't have been several dozen Klansmen at the Statehouse – there would have been thousands.

State officials probably would have joined them. City officials, too, for that matter. After all, the Klan's political punch helped elect them.

Butler University history Professor George W. Geib calls it the state's dark side. "The fact that we defeated the Klan, I think is a good thing. The fact that we had to defeat the Klan is a reminder there is a dark side."

And that makes it one of the top events to affect the city this past century.

In the aftermath of a world war, people remained suspicious of anything foreign. People also worried about changes sweeping through society. Indianapolis, a city that prided itself on being 100 percent American, seemed ripe for the Klan's warped message: It stood for what was good for America. It was a message that spread like wildfire.

The Klan opened its first Indiana chapter in Evansville in 1920, The Encyclopedia of Indianapolis notes, and quickly established chapters in every county. D.C. Stephenson, a salesman, arrived in Evansville from Oklahoma and became involved with the organization.

In 1922, Stephenson moved to Indianapolis, where he was named Grand Dragon of Indiana and 22 other states. Membership in the Klan exploded to about 250,000 statewide. In Indianapolis, as many as 40 percent of all native-born white men in the city paid $10 to join.

M. William Lutholtz, whose book Grand Dragon: D.C. Stephenson and the Ku Klux Klan in Indiana detailed the life of the Klan leader; points out that Stephenson received commissions on new members and became wealthy. He purchased a large home in Irvington.

The Klan quickly became the largest social organization in Indianapolis and dominant force in the city from 1921 to 1928. Lutholtz notes that Stephenson's presence at a July 4, 1923, Klan rally at Kokomo drew an estimated 10,000 to 50,000 people. Catholics, Jews and blacks became the target of the Klan here. However, it was Catholics who drew the most attention. Lutholtz noted there were about 32,000 Catholics in the city. "It was commonly believed that Catholics owed their first loyalty to the pope in Rome, not to the president of the United States."

Many Midwesterners believed Catholics were just waiting for orders from the pope to revolt and claim the country for the Church of Rome, he said.

The Klan emerged as the dominant party in the May primary in

1924. To celebrate, an estimated 25,000 Klansmen, women and children gathered at the Indiana State Fairgrounds. Later, some 6,500 Klansmen and their supporters paraded through Downtown while a crowd of 75,000 to 100,000 lined the streets. A Klan newspaper trumpeted the organization's election successes: "Protestant Ticket Sweeps State" and "National Papal Machine Smashed," it proclaimed in 1924. Political candidates openly supported by the Klan were elected to the offices of mayor, City Council and Board of School Commissioners in 1925. Klan-supported candidates also controlled the legislature and governor's office. However, it was a short-lived victory.

Stephenson was arrested and convicted of second-degree murder charges in the death of Madge Oberholtzer. She was a young Statehouse worker whom Stephenson began dating in 1925. He was sentenced to a long prison term.

The Indianapolis Times received a Pulitzer Prize in 1928 for its reports on the Klan's involvement in bribery and corruption of government officials. Political scandals led to the undoing of the city's mayor and the governor at the time, and interest in the Klan declined abruptly.

Down, but not necessarily out: Smaller groups bearing the Klan's name continue to find a home in Indiana.

Home to Hardscuffle and All That Jazz

Summer 1934

Miss Myrtle Allison had died from a stroke last week and they kept her on ice until her kinfolks could drive up from Florida.

* * *

"Grandma, why is Aunt Myrtle in a Halloween costume?"

Those robes were important to her ten years ago when she was a big officer in her ladies society.

"What's the big red cross for? Did she volunteer?"

"She wasn't in the Red Cross. Aunt Myrtle was not a nurse. She was just a regular homemaker like me and your momma."

* * *

"Lou Ann told me she was to be buried in her Klan Robes."

"Will they keep the casket closed?"

"God only knows. I hope so. They got them out of her closet and that's a good thing. I for one will be glad when they're gone forever. She has caused our family enough trouble for ten Klansmen."

* * *

"Joe if the word gets back to your church in Dayton you will get fired. They should have cremated her."

"Maybe she was too hot to handle."

"Very funny."

* * *

"We're assembled here today to pay our last respects to Miss Myrtle Allison, a devoted Christian and a leader in her community..."

Chapter One

Ezra and Lilah
Saturday' September 8, 1934

Ezra Temple, teacher, musician, father of a four and half year old and husband to the beautiful but temperamental Lilah, was stumbling his way up Nigger Hill on Hardscuffle Road to the shack that was his home.

"Sheee–it," The screen door caught the soft spot at the back of his ankle and the pain inflicted on the soft tissue of his ankle sent a sharp ache up his leg. He paused shortly, absorbing the blow as he called, "Hey Lilah are you about ready to go?"

The Temples were invited to a black tie affair given by Mayor Randolph Roberts for the bluestocking elite of Fort Anthony in anticipation of the formation of the Fort Anthony Symphony orchestra. The Mayor was a very enlightened old line Republican politician whose father, a New York native, had fought in the Civil War.

"Go where?" was the call from the little shed room that had been added for a temporary nursery the year before last. When Delilah Love Temple turned up pregnant they promptly married to avoid any blot on the reputation of either family. Ez and Lilah met in Nashville at the New Era Club when he was on the road with a band out of Louisville. She was attracted to his light skin and talent in music. She loved to dance. He was attracted to her tall slim but muscular and shapely figure, her lovely hair, the fine features of her face. For him, she was well-nigh perfection. She was only a slight shade lighter than he was but he had inherited the nappy hair from his daddy. He hated his hair and wished he were bald!

"To the Mayor's party," shouted Ezra Nehemiah Temple the new Associate Professor of Music at Western Indiana State Teachers College. Ezra had come to Fort Anthony as organist at the church of his great-uncle, Bishop Hannibal Caesar Hayes of the New Awakening Baptist Church in the Fort Anthony community of Nigger Hill.

"I ain't going, and I told you I wasn't going the first time you said anything about it. You go and flirt with them rich white ladies. You ain't nothing but Uncle Tom in a black tie! Mark my words when you put on that fancy white jacket they'll be givin' you drink orders!"

"This is a fine honor for my school and for my students. I think I have two or three who could audition and even have a chance of making it. Just think if I can get auditions for a couple of my best students what a break that would be for everyone!"

"Break hell, we need a break with enough money to buy groceries and milk for your son. You been here almost two years and no more money."

"We are in a depression Lilah. I'm dang lucky to have a job. They will pay me more as I prove my value to the school and the students. Young Ezra will never go hungry as long as I can teach, play the organ and do a gig of two on the weekends."

Associate Professor Temple was accomplished on the keyboard and on percussion instruments, most strings and could sweet talk a clarinet into heaven. He had played with road bands, in colored joints, dance halls and white country clubs across most of the South and the Midwest.

"I've got to go. Did you press my white shirt? Where is my white jacket? Are my black shoes shined?"

"Who do I look like? Deford Bailey! I don't shine shoes but here is your white shirt and bow tie."

"Who is that?"

"Oh, you remember the little harmonica player the evening we met? He is a shoe shine boy in Nashville."

"Sure you don't want to go?"

"Hell no. I have to look after your son. We may not be heah when you get home."

Ez had heard all that before and just let it go. There was no sense starting something that endangered his opportunity to be a part of the life of his son. He knew his manhood was tried each time he failed to respond. He also knew it took an unusual amount of strength to give up a little manhood in exchange for living up to his marriage vows!

Ez hitched a ride across town on a market wagon. When he arrived at the Mayor's residence, the party had not begun. He had been so caught up in his own agenda that he had paid no attention to the time and arrived not sociably late but "unsociably" an hour early. He knocked and was greeted by the mayor's butler and man for all reasons, Elder Ed Ricketts. Ed was a member at the New Awakenings Baptist Church and greeted Ez with "Well, if it isn't Professor Temple at the teachers, college. I did not know you were going to entertain us tonight. I look forward to hearing you do your stuff."

Ez retained his normal aplomb and calmly told Elder Ricketts that he was honored to be a guest of the Mayor and looked forward to helping with the new Symphony Orchestra.

"You are a little early. Why don't you have a seat in the library and I will get you a glass of tea."

"How early?" Ez asked.

"Oh, about an hour, but you're welcome here at any time. And I surely look forward to introducing you to Mayor Roberts and his lady."

Chapter Two

Randy and Rose
Saturday, September 8, 1934

"Randolph, tell me about the young colored man who was at the Symphony reception tonight."

This was Rose Beckham Roberts' first lady of Fort Anthony and a native of Connecticut where she met Randy Roberts when he was a student at Yale. The Beckham's were an old Yankee family with an ancestor, Oliver Wolcott, who had signed the Declaration of Independence. The Beckham's of the 19th century were abolitionists, and it is clear that Rose has deep sympathies for persons of color.

"He is an instructor at the teachers' college. Dr. Trotman suggested I invite him, so I did. Do you think his presence was distracting?"

"Oh, quite to the contrary, he is very charming and really gave the ladies something to talk about except how hard good help is to come by. He told me he is a teacher, a professor."

"He plays organ at the negro Baptist church and I understand he also sits in with bands that come into Indianapolis," answered Randolph. "I don't think he is a professor. After all he just went to work over there a couple of years ago."

"Well, he acted like a professor to me, and when he sat down at the piano after the others had left, he was very deft and lots of the girls enjoyed it."

"He may teach a little bit. I think Trotman wanted to have a colored on the staff, so he hired this fellow."

"Perhaps we can hire him to play at one of our musicals this winter." Rose responded impishly.

The winters in northwest Indiana are long; the days are short; and the First Lady did her part to enliven the long evenings in Fort Anthony.

Chapter Three

Meeting with the President
Monday, September 10, 1934

The walk to the office of President Frank Trotman was a nice opportunity to enjoy the late summer day on the campus of Western Indiana State Teachers College. The leaves were still green and the grass was lush on the well-kept lawns at the college. There is something different about the Midwest, he mused.

Having grown up on a college campus, Ez was no stranger to the mores of the environment in which he found himself. He knew that a call to the President's office was not a good sign. He had not confided in Lilah of the challenge that he could be facing on this day.

He was greeted by President Trotman's secretary, Barbara Ann Smith. "Come in, President Trotman is expecting you."

"Well, that was friendly enough," he thought.

"Good Morning, Ez." It was Frank Trotman, a larger than life figure with bushy gray hair and a bulbous nose who intimidated his faculty and staff. But not Ez. He had grown up at the knee of a college head and knew they were not perfect and their bark was barely related to their bite.

"Morning Mr. President. A lovely reception last night. I am honored to have been included. Mrs. Trotman looked especially handsome. You are a lucky man to have such a splendid helpmate in the tough assignment you have."

"Yes, she's a fine woman. She tells me you entertained the ladies on the piano after the big money people gathered in the Mayor's study."

"Yes, I did. Was that a mistake?"

"Well, you were a guest and it might have been better to let the hired pianist finish up the evening's entertainment."

"But her music was dull as ditch water. I mean how many ways can you play Clare de Lune and still call yourself entertaining?"

"Ezra, we are breaking new ground here and you are the plow point. Stay sharp."

"Yes sir, Mr. President."

"That's all Ez. Have a good day."

No matter how many times he was requested to play more of his jazz and ragtime piano tunes, Ez Temple refrained from doing so—until he left Fort Anthony for greener pastures.

Chapter Four

Later that Day
Monday, September 10, 1934

"Mr. Mayor, Fred Trotman."

"I got the boy straightened out."

"Good Idea."

"Call me any time you have a suggestion."

"Sure will."

Fred Trotman and Randy Roberts had become close friends and confidants since Fred came to give leadership to the school. The college president was on the bank board and Randy was a close adviser and member of the board at the school. They were aware of the history of the Klan in Indiana and persons in positions of leadership played the race card with care and caution.

Ez had never experienced such a subtle dressing down before, not from a teacher, or a choral director, or a bandleader, certainly not from Lilah. Lilah was as subtle as an avalanche. They had asked him to play. He had played at The Indiana Dunes Country Club before, and he knew he was good entertainment and thought the party needed some, for sure. His jazz licks and the ragtime music of Scott Joplin was the rage among white people as well as colored. What had he done that brought on his visit with Fred Trotman?

It was a pleasant evening and Randy walked the five blocks home rather than catch a ride with his assistant, Roberta Cummins, or have

Elder Ricketts bring the car around.

"Rose, I talked to Fred Trotman and he warned that colored boy he hired over at State to watch his step around here."

"Randolph why did you get into that? He didn't hurt anything and he spiced up a dull party."

"Well, Rose, I saw him flirting with some of the white women and I don't care for that kind of uppity business."

"Randolph Williams Roberts, you are Mayor of this town and Chairman of the Bank board and your job is to bring us all together and build this town into a place where every body can feel a part of it! Now get off your high horse and do your job!"

Well, rats, Randy thought as he pondered his action. Why he felt compelled to tell Rose of his call to Trotman was still a mystery to him. He ate a cold supper alone and got the cold shoulder when she arrived home after a late bridge game at the club.

Chapter Five

That Evening on Hardscuffle
Monday, September 10, 1934

Ezra was an only child; talented, with a fragile ego and sensitive to his relationship with his white superiors. He had grown up watching his daddy, Job and President Eakerly in a relationship of equals even though there was a racial divide but neither man gave it a thought.

"Lilah, I don't know whether this job will work out or not. I am gonna give it till the end of the year and see."

"What happened, did the black tie get you in trouble the other night? Did the suave Professor Temple run his boat onto rocky ground?"

"It's not a big deal but I'm gonna look around."

The next day Ez went down to the telegraph office and sent a wire to ZD Eakerly.

Two days later Dr. Eakerly chased him down at a phone in the anteroom of President Trotman's office.

"He's fine. Sorry you had so much trouble getting me on the telephone.

They don't have but three on the whole campus here at WISTC.

Thanks for calling.

I need to talk to you about a few things."

"No, it's not Lilah. She is expecting again, however."

"Just fair, she did not want to get pregnant but that's life, I told her. She'll live through it."

"I'm not sure. I don't feel comfortable here. My students and I get along fine. I am the only music faculty member, so I am my own department head. I am also the only colored member of the faculty here and that brings a lot of pressure."

"Well, I am coming down to Kentucky over Christmas break and I would like to talk to you if you could set aside some of your time for me."

"No, maybe a morning meeting in your office. I need some serious advice."

"Thanks Mr. President."

Chapter Six

The Christmas Trip
December 21, 1934

Lilah told Ez that she is not looking forward to visiting Ez's parents in Richmond over Christmas. It is a long bus ride through Indianapolis, Louisville and on to Lexington where Job would meet them in the old state truck that he drove around the campus. It's a 1927 T-model Ford and she could imagine how undependable it had become. She is seven months pregnant and not carrying the baby comfortably. It would be a rough ride, but she knew how much Ez wanted to see his parents and visit old friends on the campus of Eastern Kentucky Agricultural School. After the baby came, they could arrange for a visit to her momma next summer. Gallatin, Tennessee was just a few hours south of Louisville and the bus went down 31-E in about half the time.

While sensitive to his own feelings and fears he seemed oblivious to those of Lilah and their second child.

By December 20th, Ez had completed his responsibilities to his students, and they would not be back until January 3rd. If he and Lilah returned by the thirtieth he would be ready for the new session.

They boarded the Trailways Bus in Fort Anthony headed to Indianapolis where they would catch a Greyhound to Louisville and change buses to Lexington.

An early snow in central Indiana slowed traffic so that the bus to Louisville was late arriving. They spent most of the night in the bus station sitting in the corner on their luggage. By the time the next bus arrived and they boarded for Louisville, Lilah was complaining of back pains. After the scary seven hour ride to Louisville, they arrived in time to get a bite to eat at the colored-only lunch counter. Since living in Western Indiana, the memory of segregation was just a memory. However, the vegetable soup was hot and tasty. The trip to Lexington was down dark narrow roads and was uneventful except that Lilah continued to experience something like birth pains and a sore back. She became scared.

"Does yoah daddy know when we will be in Lexington? Will he be there when we get there? What time is it? Do you have anything left to eat in that sack?"

Little Ezra was the apex of good humor during the ordeal. Big Ez held him all the way and kept his food ready whenever he wanted to eat. Ez felt sorry for Lilah and wished a thousand times they had not attempted to make the trip.

About the time they pulled into the bus station in Lexington she gripped Ez's arm.

"This baby is coming tonight."

Ez had feared these words all day. The trip was long and hard and it was unfair of him to ask her to do this.

"O, God," he prayed, "not now, not on this bus. Please Lord, I need some help."

The bus pulled in about the time he finished his prayer and there was Job waiting for them.

Chapter Seven

Rose and Eleanor
Friday, December 21, 1934

Rose Beckham Roberts was an active member of the Women's Missionary Society at the First Methodist Church in Fort Anthony. The society meets every Tuesday. Eleanor Trotman was in her circle and the program chairman for this year's monthly meetings.

Over a cup of hot tea, she and Rose planned the program for the spring musicale, an event which they all looked forward to.

"I think we should have that young colored man from the Teachers College join us for a piano concert. He plays the organ at old Hannibal Hayes church and he might be interested in showing us what he could do on both."

Eleanor was reminded of what Fred had told her about his meeting with Ez Temple. "I don't know Rose. He may be a troublemaker."

"What do you mean a troublemaker? He seems to be a lovely young man and I think we should encourage him to get out in the community and share his talents with us. Perhaps he could bring some of his students along as well."

"Are they all colored?"

"Of course not, you should know that. Your husband is still president over there, isn't he?"

"Yes, certainly, but I hear he has organized some kind of 'jazz' group and the faculty is not too pleased."

"Well, we are not the faculty and I think the Women's Missionary Society of the First Methodist Church of Fort Anthony, Indiana, should be concerned with encouraging intelligent young colored people to move into places of prominence wherever and whenever they can."

"Well, I'll ask Fred what he thinks."

"Eleanor Trotman, if you say one word to Fred about this I'll wring your neck. We can choose whoever we want to be on our program."

"Well, Fred told me that Randolph had called him back last summer and told him he better watch the young man, he could be a troublemaker."

"Eleanor, he is a musician and a good one. There is not a mean bone in his body. All he wants to do is play his music and teach our young people to do so as well."

It was a cold December day outside and the hot tea was not enough to warm the chill that set the tone for the meeting of Circle 4 of the Women's Missionary Society of the First Methodist Church of Fort Anthony, Indiana. Later that afternoon Rose called the bank.

"Mr. Roberts, please."

"The Missionary Society went fine, Thank you! "

"Randolph Roberts you are a meddling fool and you better leave that young colored teacher alone. You call Fred Trotman and tell him you made a mistake and you think he ought to be given every opportunity to show off his talent and make the music program at that damn college one of his top priorities. Don't come home tonight until you have done that and I mean it!"

"Crap, I think she hung up! Rose, what is going on? Rose–Rose."

Chapter Eight

Job and Esther
Saturday, December 22, 1934

Job had never seen Little Ez, his grandson and he behaved like a silly grandpa at the sight of him.

"Well, how is everybody feeling?" he asked graciously.

Lilah said, "I feel bad and need to go to the hospital. I think this baby is coming now!"

"Can we find a hospital where they will check her out at this time of night?" Ez asked with a frantic voice. He knew they were in trouble.

"Can't she wait till we get back to the school? I can call Dr. Eakerly and he can have Dr. Howley meet us at the clinic."

"How long will it take to get there?" Lilah asked.

"Maybe 45 minutes, maybe an hour; I just don't know about around here."

"Well, let's hurry," responded an embittered Lilah. She was becoming very upset at the manner in which the men looked upon the birth of a baby. For Lilah, it was life or death. For Job and Ezra, it was a bother.

Job did try to make Lilah comfortable in the front seat while Ez and little Ezra covered up with a tarp and some blankets in the bed of the truck. Ez fashioned a crib from their luggage and the mattress of the bed with an old pillow Job had brought with him for that purpose. Because it was a state truck, they stopped at the county road garage to fill up with gas, check the oil and make the phone call. This took some valuable time but Job thought it had to be done.

Lilah was beginning to moan occasionally and even Job became frightened at the prospects of giving birth to a premature baby in the front seat of a Model-T pickup truck. A light chilling rain began as they were furiously driving through horse country and into the hills of Eastern Kentucky. Towns came and went as the little truck gave all it had. It had been a little over an hour since the Greyhound Bus had arrived in Lexington.

"How far is it Job?" groaned Lilah.

"Just a few minutes," answered the driver of the precious cargo.

"I think my water just broke or I peed all over myself," said the embarrassed little girl, no longer the self-assured bossy woman who had taken his son away from his family.

"Oh, my Gawd," lamented Job. "Please Lord, get us to the clinic in a hurry." He spoke loudly as if the Lord could hear him better if he shouted the words.

"Keep your knees together," he pled with Lilah, as if she could control what was about to happen.

"Keep my knees together, hell; put your foot on the gas and get me to a hospital," she shouted back at Job.

As Job rounded the curve into Richmond, Lilah went into spasms and screamed, "Help me! Please somebody help me! I'm having this baby now!"

"Hold tight!" Job screamed back and the old T-model lurched to a stop in front of the school clinic at Eastern Kentucky Agricultural School. Dr. Howley was waiting.

Chapter Nine

A Family Tragedy
Sunday, December 23, 1934

The trip to Gallatin, Tennessee was a long hard one.

The pine casket was secured in the bed of the old Model-T truck. Job was driving. They left Little Ezra behind with his grandmother Esther since Ez did not want to get into a big discussion with Lilah's mother about who would raise the boy until his father could arrange to take him home, wherever home might be.

Delilah Love Temple had given premature birth to a girl at the door to the clinic. Doctor Howley did what he could but his help was too late in coming. The premature birth of a child was not something easily dealt with at a school clinic in the hills of Eastern Kentucky.

Esther had given Lilah a sponge bath, since they had no shower. She donned clean garments and was brought to the bedroom Ez had occupied for 18 years. The house was clean, neat, and warm from the grate in the spare room and the great "Warm Morning" stove in the parlor.

Having a "Warm Morning" was a sign of prosperity and Job had just a little. He still had work at school, lots of it. Esther was teaching school and taught music to the children at church, which would, on occasion, earn her something for the table or a silver coin every now and again. She had taught son Ezra to read music and play piano and some violin before he was 5 years old.

Two days after the fatal ride to Richmond, Kentucky, Lilah had become comatose and the young doctor they had called in was unable to explain her malady. Quickly, Dr. Howley came back with young Dr. Herbert and could do no better. Sadly, Lilah died that day. A clot had formed and gone to her brain.

Job and Esther wondered why they did not advise Ez to stay put until the baby came. Job knew he could have borrowed the large, faster Peerless from Dr. Eakerly and perhaps he did not need to stop for gas-he should have tended to that earlier. These and other thoughts of guilt filled their minds.

Ezra was outwardly stoic about the entire experience. It was he who felt the need to talk to ZD Eakerly. It was he who arranged the bus trip that snowy day. It was he who arranged for Job to pick them up in Lexington. It was he who made the decision to go on to the clinic at Eastern Kentucky Agricultural School. Moreover, he refused to let her abort the child when she discovered her unwanted pregnancy. It was his fault and he was paralyzed with remorse. Nevertheless, he was not going to turn Little Ezra over to some woman he hardly knew.

It was a long Christmas Eve funeral service. The wake the night before had been hell. The two men slept in the bed of the truck where the casket had been.

Delilah Love had been a very popular girl at the Preston Taylor High School in Gallatin. She was a regular attendee at the Church of God in Christ and sang in the choir. Her mother was a deaconess who had raised her without any help. Her father had died in France in the war. Lilah had remembered him only faintly. To the community around the church and school where she was raised, Lilah was a princess, her mother a queen and her father a hero.

Where was Lilah's son? Why didn't Ez bring him? Who is going to look after him? How did Lilah die?

Her postcards did not mention the she was expecting. After four or five prayers, two sermons, one altar call, a eulogy, eight hymns and much moaning and "amening," Ez and Job were ready to escape this place. The local church people could bury her in their cemetery.

When they finished the last verse of "Beulah Land" and the preacher was offering the benediction they slipped out a side door, cranked up the Model T and left Gallatin for Nashville. Job and Ez were hopeful to experience the comfort of the home of Dr. W.O.Palmer. He was a classmate of Job at Tuskegee who had later followed his star into music and was leader of the band and professor of Music at Tennessee State Agriculture and Industrial School.

Could it really be Christmas Eve?

Chapter Ten

On to Nashville
Monday, December 24, 1934

Day turned into night as they drove the old truck down 31-East towards The Athens of the South. Nashville, Tennessee was the home of sixteen institutions of higher learning and took its nickname seriously. Nestled in a giant bowl, the coal fired industries, the home grates and "Warm Morning" stoves, which were loaded each night with large lumps of cheap coal, spewed a heavy blanket of gray coal dust that hovered above the bowl and choked the population all winter long.

As Ez and Job approached from the northeast, they could hardly see the lights of the city. All the new neighborhoods, built since the great tornado of 1926 had raked East Nashville nearly to the ground, were electrified. Gone were the gaslights and coal oil lamps of the past. It was not until the two travelers were inside the perimeter of electrification that their could they see the evidence of the modern city Nashville was becoming.

They asked for directions to Fisk University, Esther's alma mater. They knew that Tennessee A&I was not far awayfrom Fisk. The haze became worse as they drove out Jefferson Street to look for a place to stay the night. They would go to the school and find Bill in the morning.

The turrets of Jubilee Hall were only slightly visible from their room in the colored-only hotel across the street. The Hall was financed with funds raised by the Jubilee Singers on their world tour across

Europe and much of America. It was a landmark for the little campus and a focal point of pride for the colored citizens across the region. Fisk was founded after the Civil War to help educate the newly enfranchised citizens, all children of slavery.

The next morning Job and Ez fortified themselves with a big breakfast in the kitchen of the proprietress of the hotel.

Miss Sara Daniels was a small but talkative granddaughter of a brick-making freedman who used the local river clay for his trade.

"My Pa fired many of the brick used in Jubilee Hall and built this old building from bricks he had made with his own hands. He fired the lime for the mortar from mussel shells found in the creek bed down there where he dug the sand. He was a fine man and a good builder. His motto was 'A boy can start a job. It takes a man to finish one up.' My brother Bob Jr. went to A&I where he learned a little engineering and drafting. He's a builder too."

A&I was just a mile or so west of Fisk and they soon found themselves in the boiler room office of the building superintendent.

Yes, of course he knew W.O. Palmer. Dr. Palmer was off campus for a few days but he would find him if possible.

Had they forgotten it was Christmas Day?

Chapter Eleven

Christmas Day
Tuesday, December 25, 1935

The mayor of Fort Anthony, Indiana, gave an annual Christmas Open House and brunch on Christmas Day for all the municipal employees and their families. The bank paid for it but they were all customers of the bank. His opponents sniped at his Honor with the accusation that employment by the city was contingent on having a savings account in the First Bank and Trust. Not so said the Mayor and that was that. A city job was a plum during this time of bread lines and broken lives. No employee complained and three percent interest on savings was a good investment. Every employee had a savings book and five percent a week went into savings. It was a good deal.

This year the mayor invited the faculty and staff at the Teachers College to join them. The school was a good customer of the bank and Randolph Roberts wanted to keep their business. He was nearing the end of his fourth term and he liked the dual roles.

All the employees came: department heads, street sweepers, waterworks mechanics, teachers, professors and the President of the College, Fred Trotman.

"Where's the young colored man who teaches music over at the college?" queried Randolph Roberts of Fred Trotman.

"I understand that he took his wife and son down to Richmond, Kentucky to see his folks".

"I didn't know he was married; and with a son?"

"Yes, Ezra Nehemiah Temple, Jr. Pretty fancy wouldn't you say?"

"Did you follow up on my last call about my retake on the situation?"

"Yeah, I'm gonna talk to him about it when we negotiate contracts next month."

"What do you mean next month? Rose is hot as a fox in a forest fire that I called you in the first place. Then Eleanor got her all stirred up and I better bring her some good news soon!"

"Don't worry. I'll deal with it."

"I am counting on it, Fred."

Randolph Roberts could not afford to upset him or he could lose all those votes, and the account as well. Or perhaps lose Rose in the process. Few knew that Rose's father sat on the bank board as a majority stockholder. If Randolph lost Rose, he lost his job and his power.

Rose approached her husband with a grin, "Well, is Fred going to do it?"

"Yes," he answered hopefully.

Chapter Twelve

True Son of "Job"
December 25, 1934

"What have we done? Daddy, do you know it's Christmas and we were in such a hurry to get out of Gallatin that we came here and Momma does not know where we are or what we are doing. Dang, what am I thinking about? Little Ezra won't have any Santa Claus and he understands a little about it. What will I do? What will we do?"

Ezra was spitting out the words and nervous as a cat in a room full of rocking chairs. "Oh Lord, I lose my wife and it's my fault. I lose my daughter and it's my fault. I have taken you away from Momma on Christmas and I have forgotten about Little Ezra."

His soul was filled with rage and the object of his rage was himself.

"Ez, calm yourself. I told Momma before we left that we would most likely not be back for Christmas. We had a job to do and we have done part of it. She knows we will get in touch some way."

"Mr. Boiler Man is there a telephone on this campus that is hooked up today? I gotta call my Momma."

"I don't have one down here. Go up to the Ad Building and check out the pay phone inside the front door."

It was a long hike up the hill to the administration building. When they got there only one of the eight doors was unlocked and the pay phone was not working. Someone had jerked the ear piece out of the socket. The walk helped Job to settle Ez down and explain that it was not the end of the world that they were not at home, but when they returned to the old truck they were both in tears.

The drive along Centennial Boulevard and Jefferson Street toward town seemed like an eternity. There was a hollow place in their insides which neither food nor drink could fill. These last few days had been too much to endure. Job prayed while he drove. He prayed for rest. He had never been so tired. Neither man spoke, they went directly to a room in the hotel and fell on the big bed and went to sleep exhausted, mentally, physically and spiritually.

It was Christmas and they had a room in an inn.

Esther had begun to worry. Job had told her that he was not sure when they would get back and not to mention Christmas to Little Ezra. They would celebrate the birth of the Blessed Saviour when they were able to return. She had not heard from them so she walked up the hill to the President's residence.

A servant answered the door, "Well, hello, Miss Esther. Merry Christmas to you and yours."

"And Merry Christmas to you too, Vashti. Is the President or Miss Rebecca in?"

"They are resting. Can I help you? Was Santa Claus good to you Little Ezra?" She noticed the tears in Esther Temple's eyes. "What's wrong, Miss Esther? Did the services in Gallatin go all right? Did Job and Ez get back in time for Christmas?"

"Vashti, I don't know the answer to any of those questions. I haven't heard from Job or Ez, and I thought they might have called ZD or left a message here."

Esther was nervous and concerned about little Ezra and what Vashti had said about Christmas. She whispered to Vashti "Little Ezra doesn't know what today is. We are going to wait for his daddy to come home."

"Oh, I'm so sorry, Miss Esther; let me ask Early if he took a call from your men."

Esther was still standing in the foyer holding onto Little Ezra so he would not break anything, when Early, a tiny black man with a rim of white hair around his large bald spot appeared. He was the smallest man she had ever seen who was not a dwarf.

"Miss Esther, I haven't heard a word and I am sure that Mr. ZD hasn't heard nothing or he would a sent me down to your place to tell you. I promise you that when Mr. Job calls I will be down there like a duck on a June bug. You can count on that, Miss Esther."

"Much obliged Early and M-e-r-r-y C-h-r-i-s-t-m-a-s" she spelled out the seasonal greeting. "Thanks, Vashti, sorry to bother you. Say hello to Sam for me."

She headed back down the hill to the home she and Job had shared since coming to Eastern Kentucky Agricultural School sixteen years ago. They did not have a sign of holiday ornamentation around the little house.

Job woke up about two o'clock and walked down the hall to the bathroom. He came back to find Ez still asleep, so he went searching for Miss Sara. She was in her little parlor. It was decorated with a small Christmas tree. A few ribbons and gift-wrap were in evidence.

"Well, did you find your friend out at A&I? Don't 'spect so today. Them teachers take a lot of time off. When they do work, they don't do no real work. I am on duty all the time. Running a hotel is hard work. I only know about hard work. You didn't find him did you?"

"No, not yet."

"Did you call him up?"

"Couldn't find a phone."

"If you will take me over to my brother Bob's house, he's got a phone and a phone book, too. He knows most of those folks out there and he can help you find him."

Bob lived on Jo Johnson Street. in a pleasant, two-story, four-square, brick house with green wooden shingles in the gables and an airy front porch.

Bob answered the door with a happy "Merry Christmas! Come in, come in. Who have you got with you; one of your guests?"

Sara gave her younger brother a quick hug and said,"Yes, he and his son have rented a room for a day or two and he needs to find somebody from out at the state school-your alma mater."

Job jumped in quickly. "I'm Job Temple from Eastern Kentucky Agriculture, and we are attempting to locate an old friend who is on the faculty at A&I. Do you know W. O. Palmer?"

"Man, yeah, everybody knows W.O. Most likely, he's got a gig at one of the country clubs tonight for dance or something but I'll give him a call."

Bob dialed the number "Main 1196." Bill's wife answered the phone."Hello India, Bob Daniels...I'm fine, I have a friend of Bill here who needs to see him." "She wants to know your name."

"Tell her that Job Temple from old Tuskegee times is in town and I want my son to meet him."

"She says hold on."

"Hey Bill, here's an old friend of yours," Bob handed the phone to Job Temple.

"W.O. this is Job Temple...Yeah, we were in Kappa Psi together... Yeah, I am at Eastern Kentucky Agricultural School. Doing a little farming, not much...Say, W.O. have you got a minute this afternoon, I want you to meet my boy...Well, we must to get back to Richmond. It is complicated but I'll tell you when I see you...Okay, see you in a few minutes."

Bob Daniels explained that Bill Palmer lived just around the corner and gave him a house number. Job thanked him and drove around the corner to see Dr. Palmer.

Ez woke up with a start. "Dad—Dad Daddy where are you?"

He felt like a lost child. In a strange town, no phone, no friends, and now his dad, his only true friend in the world, had left him without a note or a sign or anything.

He walked down the hall to the bathroom and eased down the stairs to see if Miss Sara was around. Nobody! Suddenly he felt cold and broke out in a sweat. He almost panicked but instead he went back upstairs to the hotel room and fell to his knees. He began to pray and pray. He asked for forgiveness. He prayed for his worthless soul. He prayed for Little Ezra. He prayed for his mother and dad. He prayed for Lilah, oh, how he prayed that Lilah would forgive his selfishness. He prayed again for God in Heaven to forgive him. Then he cried. He sobbed for what seemed like an hour. He could not stop. He felt sorry for himself, for what he had done, how he ran away before the graveside service. He was frightened for his soul. He said to himself—"I'm gonna burn in Hell." He said it over and over again.

Then he began, suddenly and softly to sing an old hymn:

I come to the garden alone,
While the dew is still on the roses,
And the voice I hear,
Falling on my ear,
The Son of God discloses.
And He walks with me,
And He talks with me,
And he tells me I am his own,
And the joys we share,
As we tarry there,
No other has ever known.

The lines echoed in his mind: "He walks with me and he talks with me," and a peace came over him. He relaxed and wiped the sweat from his brow and the tears from his eyes and lay still on the floor.

Moments later the door silently opened and it was Job. Ezra jumped up and said, "I'm alive. I was dead and I am alive! Praise God Almighty, I'm alive."

Job said with surprise "Are you okay, son?"

"I'm great. I've been to the valley of the shadow and I'm ready to climb the mountain. Were you able to locate Dr. Palmer?"

"Yes and he wants us to move over to his place for tonight. But he's got to play a dance this evenin'."

"Oh, Dad could I sit in, I want to play my music very badly."

"Well, it won't hurt to ask."

Bill Palmer was downstairs in his 32 B-Model Ford Sedan waiting to meet Professor Ezra Nehemiah Temple.

After introductions, Job asked if Ez could sit in.

"What do you play Ez?"

"Oh, most anything. Do you mean instrument or genre?"

"Let's start with the instrument."

"I love clarinet, but I play piano, drums and vibes."

"Well, why don't we sneak out to school and get you a licorice stick."

On the way to the Country Club, Job told Ez that he had called his mother. He called ZD's house collect and good old Early had run down to get Esther. She called him back from the phone in the front foyer and they both were reassured as to the safety of the other. They still cared very much for each other and were seldom apart. This had been hard on both of them.

"She is okay and Little Ez is fine, too."

They pulled up to the kitchen entrance of the club and unloaded the music and stands and some of the other stuff that musician's need. The club looked enormous to Ez. Indeed, it was large–reflecting the prominent part it played in Nashville society and the wealthy folks who graced its membership list. The two story white clapboard Dutch colonial fit well into the heavily treed site. The pool and tennis courts flanked the structure on the left and the splendidly groomed golf course was beyond the massive columns that framed the back doors to the spacious foyer.

The bandstand was placed in front of a large Georgian mantelpiece with a large mirror over the mantel. A multi-faceted mirrored ball hung from the ceiling and eight crystal chandeliers as well. A small balcony overlooked the floor that was ready for dancing with a little dance wax still evident. To one side was the bar; on the other side were tall French doors that opened to the cut limestone terrace used in the warmer months.

Straight ahead was a long reception hall, which looked to Ez like something out of a storybook. More chandeliers, Persian carpets, little gold chairs on each side of the hall and at the far end another finely carved mantle with a portrait of President Andrew Jackson framed in what looked from a distance like solid gold.

"I have been to the valley and now I'm ready to climb." Ez was not slumming for sure. He was about to play a Christmas Night dance for the crème de la crème of young Nashville society.

He silently prayed, "Thank you God."

While this was a special evening for Ez, it was also special for the young people. Most had been to dancing school and knew the typical foxtrot, Charleston and the waltz. Styles of dancing changed frequently so the girls had to teach the young men how to perform the latest steps. They were polite and well-behaved. The entire evening was as from a storybook.

Ez observed that some of the young men wore tailcoats with white ties and others wore regular tux coats like his back at home.

After all, he did not ride into town on the last load of watermelons. However, tonight, he wore the same white shirt, tie, and suit he had worn to the funeral. An event that seemed a lifetime away.

That night, he thrilled the young people with his work on the clarinet. Nevertheless, when the rest of the band took a break he sat down at the piano and played some ragtime, jazz and Kansas City blues. There were always those young men who liked to hang around the bandstand hiding from some girl with whom they were required to dance. He was on the mountain. He had never felt so good, so released, yet so in tune with the heavens and the God of Heaven who had endowed him with such great talent.

They loved him and he loved them back. It was a night many of them would remember for the rest of their lives.

He would.

Chapter Thirteen

The Road Back
Wednesday, December 26, 1934

India Palmer prepared an early breakfast for them and some sandwiches for the road. Over breakfast Ez and Bill Palmer took up the conversation they had cut off somewhere in the middle of the night.

"Ez, lemme tell you about bankers and college presidents. They are so busy kissing the asses of so many politicians and so many big shots that they are scared most the time to make a move. Much less a move like hiring the first colored teacher at a white school-specially at little state schools in the Midwest. Let me give you a suggestion. Ask your president for some time off to go to The University of Indiana in Bloomington to get your Masters. It is going to be a great school of music and an advanced degree from there is gonna count for something. You have talent. You have lots of talent. That guy will be so relieved he will probably pay you to go and get a place for you and Little Ezra to stay as well. Hey, teach some, play a few dates, what the hell, you've got it made. Load off on his butt, tell him you need the time to recover from your loss, which you do, that you love Indiana and if you are good enough, you would like to come back and start a real school of music at his dumpy little teachers college."

That was a lot for Ez to digest along with four eggs, country ham, fried chicken, grits and gravy, hot biscuits and apple pie. Lord have mercy, India could cook.

Job was glad they had come, but it was a lot for him to deal with, too. He knew that Bill was inclined to optimism and a little bullhockey but this was a lot to expect. He would have to cool Ez down a bit.

"Well, I guess all good things must come to an end. It has been great to see you Brother Bill and thanks for talking to Ez. I know he appreciates your advice. I don't know a bass fiddle from a bulls' butt, but I know when my old fraternity brother gives my son advice, it will be good."

They shook hands; Ez and Job hugged India Palmer and they headed to the Gulf Station to gas up for the ride to Richmond.

They filled up at the station at 21st and Acklen and headed over to the Franklin Pike to go up 31East through Gallatin and on to Richmond, Kentucky. It was well after dark when they pulled into the gravel driveway at Job's house.

Esther was waiting.

Chapter Fourteen

A Friend in Need
Monday, December 31, 1934

Dr. Eakerly was the best friend Job Temple ever had or ever would have. He was good to Esther and Ez worshipped him for his goodness and generosity. It was natural that he should ask for some of his time to review his options at this critical juncture.

ZD invited him for lunch at the Residence on the day before Ez was to go back to Fort Anthony. Of course, he knew about Lilah's death and the tragedy surrounding their lives and was tremendously empathetic towards Ez.

Ez told of his confusion about the situation in Fort Anthony, his marriage to Lilah, his tremendous guilt upon her death and his hotel room epiphany in Nashville. He told of the guilt he felt while driving back to Richmond after he had been on such an emotional high while entertaining the young people at the prep school dance. He shared Bill Palmer's advice, even his comment about bankers and college presidents.

"Ez, you are still a very young man. Life has not passed you by. What would you like to do on the first day of the rest of your life? That's where you are. This is an important crossroads and with your talent, your genes, your new faith in a Higher Power, a beautiful son and supportive family and friends; the world is truly your oyster."

"Dr. Eakerly, I guess I am not as sure of my talent as you and others may be. I am unsure what to do about my son and I must find more meaning for my life."

"My advice is simple Ez. Be open to the Spirit of God and listen to the music, the music of the Spirit. Turn on your spiritual radio and find guidance in the music that you hear there."

Ez had never heard ZD speak of anything spiritual but he was pleased with what he heard.

"Look Ez, I am getting close to retirement and the Legislature is becoming more interested in what we are doing here. Your dad has been terrific in his research and is carrying a big load otherwise. They are giving us Roosevelt money and as you well know, we need some new vehicles. The auditors tell me I can dispose of my auto and the pickup truck, and I wondered if you would like to work something out for one of them?"

Ez had never owned a vehicle before and did not want to seem nervous but asked, "What about that Dodge panel truck that Early drives back and forth to the Post Office and all?"

"That's a possibility."

"That would be ideal for me. If I start up a little group I need something to carry stuff in."

"I tell you what; if you work it out to go to grad school, it's a deal."

"Mr. President, you just told me what I need to hear. I'll write with a progress report." Ez rose from the table, went to ZD Eakerly, and gave him a big hug. ZD had been a second father to him and there was great affection between them.

It was beginning to sleet when he left the Eakley residence to walk home, but he was a man on a mission. His head was in the clouds. He was way ahead of reality, but dreamers occasionally see their dreams come true.

The ride back to Lexington was treacherous even in Dr. Eakerly's big auto. He insisted that Job take the car so that Esther and Little Ezra could see Ez off at the bus station. Santa Claus had been good to Little Ezra when Christmas finally came at the Temple house; no ashes and switches but a pull toy, some blocks and a wagon that Job had freshly painted. He was a happy child and talking up a storm. His daddy would miss him but June was not far away. Esther would take him to school with her on the school bus with the rest of the colored children.

Chapter Fifteen

Calling In a Favor
January 30, 1935

School had been in session for three weeks when Rose Beckham Roberts asked the Chairman of the Board at the bank what he had heard from the President of the Teachers College about the status of the young colored music teacher.

"He's working on it" was the terse reply.

"Well, I want a full report and soon. He has had almost a month now. You call him this afternoon. Call me back!"

That witch, he thought. She can be a pain to live with sometimes.

"Roberta, will you get President Trotman on the phone?"

"I have him on now, Randy."

He and Roberta Cummins had gone to grade school together. She was an old maid and the best secretary a man ever had.

"Are you some kind of mind reader?"

"No, Rose told me to call him when you hung up talking to her."

"Fred, things okay on campus?"

"That's good to hear. Sounds like you're busy."

"Well, Rose called just now…"

"What music program? You said he couldn't cut it."

"That's good."

"Tell you what; why don't you give him some time off, can't he come back up here a couple of days a week and teach and work on his Master's on the other days. You know Allen Willson down at The University. He will do you a favor won't he?"

"Rose, he's got it all figured out. I'll tell you about when I get home."

That night the Chairman of the board explained the dilemma faced by the President of the school to the wife of the mayor.

"Here is what Trotman told me. He is truly working on it. The boy wants Fred to give him a leave to go to the university to complete his graduate education and that will knock the heck out of his music program! The other faculty members are saying he has some kind of musical gift and that he is going to have a spring musical with our students. A little chamber orchestra of some kind and a chorus of a few of our students and the choir at his uncle's church. If he leaves, Fred will be in a bind! But, he said he will continue to work on it."

"Well, here's what you two are going to do. You are going to send him down to The University and the bank will pay for his rent and a food allowance. IU will give him a full scholarship and pay him something for teaching music. I know he is a fine musician and I hear he is a genius as a teacher. Fred will keep him on full pay that he can send home to take care of his little boy in Richmond, Kentucky. I have been looking into the tragic situation he has faced and I want you to make this happen!"

Chapter Sixteen

A Letter Home
February 21, 1935

Dear Mom and Dad,

Jesus has answered my prayers. Praise the Lord!

President Trotman has found a way to help me do everything that Dr. Palmer said I should try to do.

He contacted the headman of Indiana University at Bloomington, Indiana about me. He has arranged for me to rent a room off campus, for food on campus anytime I want to eat there, I will be paid for the classes I teach, as long as my grades are good. I get a full scholarship and I can still teach here on Mondays and Friday. They will send you my check from the college to take care of Little Ezra, and I can still direct the choir and play the organ at Uncle Hannibal's church.

Dad, ZD said something about selling the Dodge panel truck to me cheap and I need transportation to get to all the places I go. Will you ask him about that soon? I might get a loan or if you can help me, I would appreciate it.

I feel so unworthy of all the good things that are happening to me. I miss Little Ezra and I think about Lilah a lot. She was really a good person. I'm sorry things turned out the way they did. I don't think I will ever marry again. It makes me sad to reflect on that experience.

I pray for forgiveness every day. I am being showered by God's grace and I am so unworthy. Praise Jesus. All blessings surely do flow from him!

Give Little Ezra an extra hug for me. I miss him so much.

Love to all, your son."

Ez

PS- I am producing a Spring Musical on May Day. I wish you could be here. Love –E

PPS-Do not forget to ask ZD about the truck.

Ezra was filled with apprehension when he took the letter to the school mailbox. He hoped that Job would be proud of him.

Chapter Seventeen

The Father-in-Law
Early March 1935

There is always a little strain on the son-in-law when his in-laws come to town. When the father in-law is also the largest stockholder in the business, it can become nerve wracking. With the bank board scheduled to meet soon, Randy would naturally be on edge.

The Beckhams were to arrive a few days before the meeting and Rose intended to bring both of them to the spring musical if Father Beckham could refrain from smoking cigars long enough. He really enjoyed his Cuban cigars, so much so it seemed to Rose that he probably had one in his mouth when she was conceived, an image that always made her smile. He was a softhearted family man with the voice of a longshoreman-deep and gruff. She laughed at how frightened Randy was when he would come by the house in New Haven to pick her up for a date. They became friends but Randy continued to be a little intimidated by Oliver Wendell Beckham.

Ollie Beckham made his money in mining New York State minerals, slate, granite, limestone, asbestos and anything else that could be dug up and sold for a profit. Although born in New Haven, he graduated from Cornell University with a primary interest in mining, engineering, and geology. He had served in France as a Colonel in an engineering division; there, he acquired quite a reputation for demolishing bridges and all kinds of structures put up by the Kaiser's engineers. He took great pride in his work.

When he returned to the quarries and mines he had turned over to his younger brothers he found them humming along better than ever. They were producing tons of product a day for the new skyscrapers beginning to replace the ancient four story landmarks of New York City. Beckham and Fils was a going concern and he was ready to rejoin the company. They shipped carloads of asbestos to Chicago and Cleveland each week, thousands of tons of granite to New York, slate to the many factories that processed it for flooring, roofing and other construction uses, crushed stone to the highway contractors who used Beckham and Fils Portland Cement by the carload to build the growing highway system of New England. Beckham and Fils would be a cash cow for almost fifty years.

Randy was pleasantly surprised to receive this correspondence from his father-in law.

The Island Inn
Sanibel Island, Florida
Thursday February 28, 1935
Dear Randolph:

Greetings from sunny Florida, Mother Beckham and I have been pleased to be here during the cold weather being experienced by our friends in Connecticut. We miss them but not enough to go back until it warms up. We are quite pleased with the accommodations here at the Island Inn on Sanibel Island. Mr. and Mrs. Wills are a pleasant couple and we enjoy our bridge games. He and I play a little old man's tennis together, also. No golf course here, too many alligators! The food is good, the colored help is charming and the weather here in the upper tropics can't be beat. We will take the "Southern Breeze" through Louisville up to Indianapolis and you can meet us there. I will be there in time for the board meeting.

My reason for writing is to congratulate you on the good work you are doing in building better relations among the good people of Fort Anthony. In the end, it will be good for business and unless someone like you takes a firm stand and offers a hand to the young coloreds, we will be in trouble in America. Young people will be the key to domestic peace.

I look forward to meeting young Professor Temple. Rose writes her mother that he is very talented and very well spoken. I anticipate with great pleasure the opportunity to offer my congratulations to you at the board meeting in two weeks.

You are doing a fine job at the bank and we are lucky to have you continue with us.

Mother Beckham sends her best regards.

Affectionately,

Father Beckham

PS: Mother Beckham had hoped to visit with Mrs. Lindberg whom she had met at the Literary Club last year. She is disappointed but The Lindberghs left in late December for England. I do not blame them. This has been a wretched time for them and now with the trial of Hauptman it must be too much for them.

Any news on grandchildren?

OWB

“Hello Rose, —Why don’t we go up to Chicago and live it up a little this weekend?”

Chapter Eighteen

A Working Musician
Tuesday March 5, 1935

Ez was working night and day to put an impressive program together for the May Day Musical. He was invited to the Methodist Church to perform but expressed regret citing time constraints imposed by his duties at school and his church. He offered to bring some members of his choir to perform, and the ladies of the Missionary Society, led by Rose Roberts, enthusiastically accepted the choice. This added another load to the already overworked and underpaid Ezra Temple. No matter, he felt better than he had for a long time. He had always known that he was ordained for something special. But what?

He chose twelve members of the choir who committed to a tight schedule and who could get off from work to perform at the Missionary Society meeting. Performing during a weekday was not something easily arranged.

Only two men could get off work; one bass and one baritone. They worked at night at the college cleaning up the classrooms and gymnasium. He would have to teach the tenor part to Annie Dyer. She was a contralto with a fine range and could do it easily. Owen Bailey was capable of carrying some of the bass parts along with the lead bass Red Dyer, Annie Dyer's brother. The other two altos were good enough to do the job, and the other contralto could carry the whole bunch on her shoulders if necessary. His soprano section consisted of two sets of twins- one set singing Mezzo when the arrangement called for it.

The group was to be accompanied by Ladye Frances Hayes, daughter of the preacher, playing piano. Ez would conduct the whole thing. He considered bringing the string quartet from school but decided that would be too much.

Chapter Nineteen

Relaxing At the Drake
Friday, March 8, 1935

She wondered what Randy had been up to but Rose was looking forward to the retreat to Chicago. She adored New York and had visited the city twice a year since she was a teen to shop and see some shows. She was also fond of Chicago. Randy was calmer in Chicago and they enjoyed the company of one another more when they were both relaxed.

A late winter snow pelted the windshield of his Buick sedan that afternoon as they drove through Gary and into Illinois and downtown Chicago. He had thoughtfully arranged for a suite at the Drake. Rose hoped it would have a view of the lake, an astonishing scene even during the dark days of winter. It was almost seven when they checked into the hotel.

Randy was a little unsure of himself and suggested they unpack and go down to the Oak Room and have a drink and they could enjoy some wine with dinner. He had three Scotches and was totally unwound. She had a Manhattan that she sipped for the thirty minutes they were in the bar. They had decided to have dinner at the hotel tonight, and tomorrow evening they would take a cab over to the Stockyards, where he could enjoy a fine piece of Midwestern extra prime beef rare. They caught the elevator and went up to the restaurant in The Drake for dinner.

Rose had a little glow and kissed Randy in the car on the way to the top. He had lipstick on his face when the Maitre-de welcomed them to the dining room. They decided on fish and Rose said she would enjoy a glass of white wine, Randy wanted to order a bottle, but Rose discouraged him. She had plans for tonight and she did not want Randy sloppy drunk in the bed with her. The wine steward brought them a giant glass of a nice White Bordeaux. They split a Caesar salad, she ordered Sole Muniere, and he ordered Red Snapper. She loved to watch the waiter bone the fish at the table.

"How is your snapper?"

"Its fish," he said. "Do you like the wine?"

"It's lovely; has a nice bouquet and not too much bite."

"Glad you like it; want another glass?"

"No, I think this will do. If I drink too much at night I wake up and have a hard time sleeping the rest of the night."

"Mind if I have another?"

"Do I have a say in the matter?"

"Sure."

"I'd rather you didn't."

"Okay, I won't," he responded testily. Be careful he thought. I want her to have a good time tonight.

They finished the meal with a little ambrosia and some cookies. She had a cup of hot tea.

They usually took a short walk on the sidewalks around the hotel but it was cold and the wet snow was still falling. They decided to go to their room and read a bit.

Chapter Twenty

Back at Eastern Kentucky Agricultural School
Friday, March 8, 1935

"Esther did you see this letter from Ez?" asked Job. "Looks like things are falling into place for him."

"I hope so. He has had a string of bad luck losing his baby and his wife and he could use a break. He is really a good boy, Job, and I hope he can find himself."

"Well, read this. He seems to have a handle on some things anyway."

He handed the letter to Esther and she began to cry.

"Job can you believe this. I have prayed for him every day. My prayers are being answered for sure."

"I think I'll go up to see ZD and let him read it. He loves Ezra like he was his own son and I want him to read this himself."

"Wait, I want to walk with you."

"Mrs. Temple we could drive your seven passenger Peerless Sedan up the hill if you wish, madam!"

"Or, Mr. Job Temple, we could drive your 1925 Ford Pick-Up truck if you so desire.""

"That would be nice but why don't we walk and hold hands? Get your grandson bundled up and we'll go up to the Presidents Home."

It was late Friday afternoon and ZD was piddling around in his shop. He had grown up in a farm implement dealership and he loved to restore antique farm equipment. He devoted a small space to his restorations at one of the campus barns.

"Mr. President, we have something for you to read."

"Oh, the latest news from our professor, I hope?" ZD had high hopes for Ezra and was always anxious to hear any news.

Job gave him the letter and tears came to his eyes as he read it.

"I am so proud of that boy. He is going places and doing things, I just know it. I know what we will do! We will drive up to Fort Anthony and celebrate Mayday with Ez. I will drive my new LaSalle, and Job you can drive the Dodge truck."

"ZD are you sure you can do that deal with Ez? You have done too much for us already with Esther's car and my truck."

"Job, I'll do it or get it done. Don't you worry about that. Our Ez is going to be something and we are gonna help!"

Job had never seen him so overcome with joy.

Little Ezra whispered in Esther's ear. She quietly said to Job, "We have forgotten about Little Ezra."

ZD picked the child up and said "Little Ezra, we're going on a road trip to see your Daddy. Do you want to go?"

"Yes sir, Mistah ZD."

"Then we'll all go!"

They talked for a few more minutes and Job and Esther rejoiced and praised God as they walked hand in hand down the hill to their cottage.

Chapter Twenty-One

After Dinner
Friday Evening, March 8, 1935

The room was warm, so he cracked open the windows on each side of the bay window in their bedroom of the suite. They closed the transoms tightly, Randy went into his bathroom, and Rose went into hers. An unfamiliar noise came from Randy's bath. He was vomiting into the commode, sick as a dog.

This is not exactly how she envisioned the rest of the evening, but you take them for better or worse. Rose silently closed the door and changed into her gown and peignor. She had packed a book to read so she curled up on the sofa in the living room and read. In a while, the puking stopped and she could hear the shower running in his bath. She continued to read. In about fifteen minutes, Randy showed up looking a bit peeked but in his robe and pajamas and asked if she had brought a book for him.

"I brought this month's *Ladies Home Journal.* They have a special article on food poisoning which you might like to scan." Then she softened her tone, "Sorry you are not well; was it the fish?"

"Must have been. I'll feel better in the morning."

"I brought some aspirin and some baking soda if you want to take something."

She is not so bad, Randy thought. I have sure made a mess of this night. He had high hopes and he had crushed them himself.

He picked up the magazine she offered and said, "Where is the aspirin and soda? I think I'll take some and lay down; do you mind?"

"No, that's fine. Get some rest we can talk when you are better."

Talk, he thought, does she mean talk or does she mean talk talk? He hoped she would love him in the morning more than she does tonight! "Good night," he sheepishly murmured.

"Sweet dreams, darling. I'll be in after a few." She picked up her book and read two pages. She walked over to the large window overlooking the lake. The large wet snowflakes were still coming down and the street below was covered with a fresh coat of white. She thought to herself, I am almost thirty years old and no children. If we are going to start, this weekend is it. She knew she must treat him with tenderness if her plan was to work.

Chapter Twenty-Two

Call from Father Beckham
Friday Evening, March 8, 1935

"Hello, Mary Ella, this is Father Beckham is Rose there?"
"Is Mr. Roberts there?"
"Will they be in tonight?"
"When do you expect them?"
"Do you know where they are?"
"Well, where are they?"
"Why did they go to Chicago?"
"What kind of fun?"
"Well, what did she say when she left?"
"Thank you, Mary Ella. Behave yourself."
"Good bye, Mary Ella."
"What did Mary Ella say, Father Beckham."
"Not much, just enough."

Chapter Twenty-Three

Long on Desire, Short on Performance
March 9, 1935

She read until almost midnight. It was a long book and she could spend as much time as she pleased reading this weekend. Although she did not please to read the entire weekend away.

She slipped into the bedroom and went into her bathroom. As she applied the cold cream to her face, she thought about Randy and their days together in New Haven. She was a freshman at Trinity and he was a senior at Yale. She intended to major in Yale men and he was perfect. He stayed on to get his masters in finance and to pursue her. Her folks liked him and his pleasant Midwest manner of speaking. He had attended Groton, but retained a little of the small town charm she loved so well. The Midwest was home to many excellent liberal arts schools so she was not sure why he came to Yale. He said that his grandfather wanted him to be in finance and he needed to make the right connections.

He went to work at the Rockefeller Brothers' bank in New York for a couple of years before they were married, but he missed the green, green grass of Indiana and longed to return. The Presidency of the bank in Fort Anthony came open and his dad (at the suggestion of the new majority stockholder) called him about the job. He jumped at the opportunity.

They were married in New Haven and he took his bride back to a new house, a new job, a new town and the First Methodist Church of Fort Anthony. She had been raised in the Episcopal Church. The transition was not difficult as she felt it was important to support him in his work and the best way she could do that was to become active in the Methodist Church.

After many years of a happy marriage, success at work and in politics Randy was a happy man. Rose felt unfulfilled. She wanted a child and Randy had wanted to wait. She had waited enough.

She slipped between the smooth sheets under the sateen covered down comforter on the hotel bed. Randy was breathing hard but he did not snore. Soon she dozed off with concern about what tomorrow might bring.

She awoke with the bright sun pushing its way through the slits in the Venetian blinds. It looked as if it might be a gorgeous day today. She slipped into her bathroom and brushed her hair and her teeth. When she walked out, she realized the room was chilled. They had left the windows cracked for some fresh air and now it was a little too fresh.

She did not put on her robe but stuck her head into the parlor and Randy was dozing after what looked as if he had played fifty-two pickup with the Sunday papers. She went over and whispered into his ear, "Will you please come in here and get back into this bed and warm me up? It's freezing in that bedroom."

She had surprised him. He jumped up and almost saluted as he said, "Sure thing. Did I leave the window open when I slipped out earlier? I did not want to disturb you."

"Will you get in here? I want to talk to you."

He thought to himself does she want to talk or does she want to talk talk.

"Sure, anything you say." He was a little sheepish about last night.

He closed the windows.

"Will you pull the drapes too?" she asked.

"Whatever her highness wants." he replied with hope in his heart.

He slid under the covers and snuggled up to her. She had removed her gown before she got back into the bed.

They ordered a light breakfast and asked the waiter if it would be okay to light the fire in the fireplace. He said he would do it for them. He volunteered to bring up some more wood, commenting that this might be a good morning to stay close by a fire. It had become very cold overnight. The surprise snowfall had blanketed the city and it was difficult to get around town.

Randy tipped him generously and asked for some more hot tea for Rose.

They sat on the loveseat before the fire and talked intimately about their days in New Haven, skiing in the Vermont Mountains, house parties with friends at her parents' home on the Cape and the Durant Convertible coupe with the rumble seat. They had it very good and both knew how lucky they were. It was a good visit.

The fire was warm and the temptation to snuggle up before it was more than they could resist. After a minute or two he asked if he should go get the comforter. She curled up on the Persian rug with a sofa pillow under her head and simply said, "Come here, lay you head right here." She indicated to him to put his head on her right shoulder and they were transported back to the time they fell deeply in love.

They spent a little time at the Museum and came back to the hotel to dress for dinner. Randy was hungry but he was not about to make the mistake he made last night.

They went to his favorite the "Stockyards Restaurant" to eat. She ordered squab, preceded by a green salad, a baked potato with a little salt and a smidgen of butter. He ordered a generous size Eye of Rib steak with baked potato, lots of butter and a Faucon salad. They splurged on a large serving of bread pudding with rum sauce. Her wine was white and French from Bordeaux, his was Chateau Nuef de Pape, but only a glass of the red Bordeaux. It had been his father's favorite and he learned to drink red wine with his dad by his side.

The conversation that night was animated and fun as they continued to think of things in their lives before they met. She did not mention any old boyfriends and he certainly did not mention any of his amorous adventures pre-Rose Beckham.

When he excused himself to go to the rest room, he called the hotel and asked the concierge to send a car, to put some champagne in their suite and to have someone light a fresh fire in the fireplace.

They drank a glass of the excellent champagne before the fire and retired early. A couple in love with love and each other.

It was a great weekend in Chicago.

Chapter Twenty-Four

Preparing to Sing Out
March 20, 1935

The small choir worked all Sunday afternoon and after prayer meeting that night in preparation for the musicale at the Methodist Church. This performance had important social and possibly even political overtones.

Even though Indiana was what some claimed to be a "Yankee" state it was decidedly not so. Indiana was a state with strong Middle American values of thrift, close families, high ethical standards, education and a faith-filled population. They were neighborly folk who were a fine example of De ToqueVille's America. They gathered together to solve their own problems, to build their own schools, hospitals, institutions of higher learning and much of this activity was centered around the hundreds of churches which dominated the cityscapes and the small towns across the state. Their social and political decisions were informed by their deep faith in a Creator God who loves them and they in turn love their neighbor and do it by their deeds as well as their words.

But outside of Indianapolis and Gary, there were not many coloreds in the state. Fort Anthony was no exception. There were no Hispanics, a handful of persons of Middle Eastern Semitic descent and only three percent of the population of 23,475 was colored. There were less than seven hundred and fifty negroes in the whole of the County of Collier, Indiana.

A person of color had never worshipped at the First Methodist Church of Fort Anthony, Indiana. Vern Shipley was concerned that his colleagues at the Episcopal, Presbyterian and Campbellite Churches would give him a hard time and attempt to proselyte his members. His appointment by the Bishop of Indiana to this parish was a plum from which the 62-year-old minister had hoped to retire or elected Bishop. He would not be the first Bishop elected from Fort Anthony if that were to be the case. He wrote Bishop Kenworthy to seek his advice. The Bishop advised Reverend Shipley to make the best of it. He also said that if invited he would try to attend. He responded with a prompt note back to Rose Beckham Roberts the wife of the Chairman of the Board and President of the Bank and Trust Company of Fort Anthony. If the Bishop had known she was the daughter of the founder and principal stockholder of Beckham and Fils, the international mining company, he might have been more prompt and more effusive. There were times when a bishop must develop relations, which will secure his place as the leader among equals. One never knew when those times occur.

The week flew by and Wednesday evening prayer service was dedicated to the final rehearsal of the traveling choir of the New Awakenings Baptist Church. The congregation gathered in great anticipation of the program and the quality of the performance of the group.

They were not disappointed. The choir's repertoire was stretched to the limit. The bass became a basso profundo, the alto turned tenor was splendid and the mezzo-soprano was without peer. Because the director had chosen hymns from the Methodist Hymnal, some of the music was not familiar to the colored congregation but it was sprinkled with old favorites as well. The one-hour performance went by as if it was minutes. Bishop Hannibal Hayes asked God's blessings as the choir went into strange territory on the morrow as he pronounced the benediction.

Bishop Hayes was bursting with pride. However, he was hurt because the minister at the church had not invited him. That was a temporary problem. Bishop Edwin Kenworthy came by his home early on Thursday morning to offer him a ride to the church. He enjoyed the ride in the chauffeur driven sedan in which the Methodist Bishop traveled from district to district.

Chapter Twenty-Five

The Missionary Society
March 21, 1935

Word got around early on the morning of the Missionary Society meeting. Rose Roberts and Eleanor Trotman had invited the choir from the little colored Baptist church over on "Nigger Hill" to sing some songs for the Missionary Society meeting that day. Practically the only people of color to enter the New Anthony Methodist Church were there to cook and clean up the building or that was what they said. Who ever they were.

Urgent calls were received by Rose and Eleanor asking if it would be all right if they came and brought their maid or cook with them? The answer was always a pleasant "yes, but we don't have enough lunch for everybody." I'll bring a little something was the reply. "See you at around ten after our business meeting."

Rose got the feeling something out of the ordinary was about to happen today. She began to get nervous. The bishop was coming, we might not have enough chairs, we will need more tea, and on and on. What have I gotten myself into, she thought?

"Eleanor, have you received any calls from ladies wanting to attend the program?"

Eleanor is a little bit flighty sometimes.

"Well, it's exciting if you call having the bishop, a bunch of guests, some who are bringing their maids, not enough food to eat or tea to drink exciting then it should be a hell of a party."

"Yeah, but remember who did the loaves and fishes."

Rose hung up and immediately called the church, "May I speak to Dr. Shipley please?"

"Vern, this looks like it is shaping up to be a disaster."

"It's Rose Roberts. How did the word get out about our program today? I have been swamped with calls! What will we do with a big crowd?"

Rose went on, "The fellowship hall in the basement isn't set up for over sixty people maximum. We had fifty reservations from our members and we have about fifteen guests including the choir and Bishop Kenworthy. Where will we put twenty or thirty more people?"

"The bishop, my foot, they want to bring their maid or their cook with them. The Board of Stewards will have a fit when they hear about all those coloreds at their church. Pretty soon they will want to transfer their membership."

"Good, I'll quit worrying. You start praying."

"That's good to know. See you shortly."

"Goodbye preacher."

Rose thought, he had better pray hard and often. His hopes for Bishop may have been shot.

What neither Rose nor Vern understood was the history of the colored folk and the white folk gathered in the same sanctuary hearing the same sermon, same prayers and singing the same songs. Those who had come north from the slave owning parts of the South had a history of going to church with the whites. Even though they were in a gallery set apart, they were there.

Vern heard some commotion down the hall and recognized the voice of the Bishop greeting all the staff as he moved toward the Ministers study. He thought "that rascal did not tell me he was coming early." "Louise, heat some water for tea!"

Vern, strode out of his office with a gait showing all the confidence of an efficient and effective minister of the Gospel and manager of resources here at Fort Anthony First Methodist. He knew that the local bishop was always consulted about any nomination from his area and this was big, very big!

"Good Morning, Vern! You know Bishop Hannibal Hayes from the New Awakenings Baptist Church," said Bishop Kenworthy gesturing to his fellow Bishop. "Why would the Bishop think he had met him," thought Vern. He had just started up a little church for some of the coloreds in town and was a welder before then. He did not even have a college degree and God only knows who ordained him! Surely, Vern knew that not every Methodist preacher had a college degree.

"Why yes. It's good to see you again, Bishop." The Black man reached out his hand. Both of the local men knew that Shipley was not being truthful!

Dangation! He thought. Why didn't I think of that? I should have invited him over for the program. How stupid of me. He consoled himself with the thought that we each have a little clay on our feet.

Chapter Twenty-Six

The Musicale at the Methodist Church
Thursday, March 21, 1935

Randy asked, "Rose, is Mother Beckham going with you to hear the program, I forgot to ask her."

"Yes and Father is joining us as well. Could someone pick them up in about an hour? I'm late and I won't have time to come back and get them."

"Be glad to arrange it, Rose. Good luck." She gave him a light kiss on his cheek.

"I'll need it."

Rose jumped into her old roadster and headed to the church. The business meeting was dull and she was a little jumpy. She could not wait for it to end! She thought—who is doing lunch, how many chairs can we stuff in the activity room, will they prepare enough tea, enough plates, enough forks and napkins—hush, she told herself. What is to be will be. It's too late now. She calmed down. She wanted a cigarette so badly she could hardly stand it. "A nice glass of that white Bordeaux with lunch would be good too…No chance of that…I had forgotten how good Randy is in the sack," she thought as she dispelled the thoughts about the business at hand. "But," "she reflected, I'm pretty good as well…I wonder if I am pregnant. Please God I want to be pregnant...I want a little girl…Please God, I want a little girl…" She continued to lobby God until the last prayer was said ending the meeting. She did not worry about the program, the guests, the food, or any history they might make today. She had the strange almost spiritual feeling that she was indeed pregnant and that she indeed was going to have a little girl... She would ask Mother about that.

She quickly left the meeting room to check on things. Actually, she went to a little used ladies room to smoke a cigarette. Eleanor had beaten her to it.

"You skunk," she said to Ellie Trotman. "I didn't know you knew about this hideaway. Nervous?"

"A little, you?"

"A little, well let's go face the music, so to speak."

"Rose, you know this was your idea."

"Is that a compliment?" She knew it was Ellie's way of warning her of possible trouble.

"Of course," she snickered good-naturedly.

"Let's hope for the best."

They went into the activity room/fellowship hall triumphantly. It was practically empty. Only Mollie, a staff member was present.

Rose thought, "I'll bet he moved it!"

"Who moved it?"

Mollie answered, "Preacher, he moved it to the Sanctuary. Said it was going to be too crowded down here for the program and lunch, too. We're fixing the tables for lunch."

"How many?"

"Not sure. He said set up all the tables and we would make do if that was not enough."

Oh, Lord, thought Rose, what in the name of peace is going on here now? She and Ellie rushed upstairs to the Sanctuary to see it filled with almost two hundred faces--all colors of faces. The ladies with the darker faces were all in white dresses with white gloves, hats and white shoes. The pink-skinned ladies were dressed in many styles, spring suits, and Sunday dresses, some with hats, all with gloves. She panicked. She looked for Vern the preacher, the man in charge, the man who made decisions, the man who wanted to be Bishop soon. She spotted him. He was in the narthex greeting the guests as they came in the door. She walked down a side aisle and approached him.

"Oh Vern, thank you so much for taking charge. Ellie and I stopped by to powder our noses and when we went to Fellowship Hall, someone said you had moved the program to the Sanctuary. What will the Board of Stewards say?"

Vern was the essence of suave. "The Bishop suggested we make this change. It was no trouble. I was glad to cover for you and Ellie. Anything else I can do to help?" He was being uppity and she knew it.

Ellie asked, "Well, what should we do about involving the Bishop in the program?"

"I asked him to say a few words of greeting; I'll introduce him of course. Then he suggested we invite Bishop Hannibal Hayes, the Pastor from the New Awakenings Baptist Church to offer a prayer."

Rose stuttered, "T-t-that's fine. I mean thanks a lot." This thing was out of hand, especially her hand and she was glad of it. Darn, she had forgotten to invite Ezra's preacher. What kind of politician's wife was she anyway? Not very good, she judged. And the worst of it, she now owed Vern a favor. Wonder what that would be? I can't get him elected bishop. No worry, she thought. He's harmless.

Chapter Twenty-Seven

More of the Musicale
March 21, 1935

Wanting to lighten up the occasion, Rose leaned over and whispered jokingly in Ellie's ear, "Why do women wear gloves when they are out in public like this?"

"Because Emily Post says to do it, I guess."

"I can't speak for Emily Post, but I am the wife of a politician and I shake the hands of a lot of men. I don't think they wash their hands after they use the bathroom or pick their noses."

Ellie sat back silently digesting this piece of wisdom from her younger friend.

The influx of members and visitors began to slow about 10:15 and The Reverend Dr. Vernon Edwin Shipley stepped to the lectern. The Reverend Dr. Kenworthy, Bishop of the Methodist Church for the State of Indiana was seated in the first pew on the right in the aisle seat and next to him was Bishop Hannibal Hayes, the honored guest of Bishop Kenworthy.

Vern was a little nervous but very effective as he welcomed the congregation for the program today. He spoke of the great tradition of the worship of our great Creator God with song. He was brief—for a change. He then introduced Bishop Kenworthy who was no stranger to Fort Anthony as he had ordained three young Timothy's from among the members of this congregation.

The Bishop spoke from his heart on the significance of this event in the life of Fort Anthony. Spontaneously he asked the organist who had been playing softly for almost forty minutes if she could find a special hymn for the day since this was not on the program. (Nothing he was saying was on the program).

He asked all who could to rise and join him in the first verse of the hymn "In Christ there is no East or West."

In Christ, there is no east or west
In him no south or north
But one great fellowship of love
Throughout the whole wide earth.

After the hymn, which was unfamiliar to the guest choir but was sung with great fervor, he asked Bishop Hayes to join him on the podium. He introduced the colored minister to the assembly as if they were old friends. Then he asked him to come to the lectern and lead in prayer.

Surprisingly, Bishop Hayes instead told the story of another Ezra he had known in his growing up church in Alabama. How Uncle Ezra, as everyone called him, always prayed for the children. I suppose he thought that our only hope was in our children. Uncle Ezra prayed for "the children here today, for those we are expecting soon and all those children of the future, those children who would people this earth for all the times ahead, until the Lord returns."

One little girl sitting with her mother in the balcony, upon hearing the deep bass voice of the speaker, said in a voice heard by all those around her, "Is that God?"

"No, Julia Anne. He is a friend of God and knows him well."

"Sure sounds like God to me."

He then delivered a brief but stirring prayer for all the children of God who were here today and those who might be there when Christ came again. There were amens' said all over the audience, including Bishop Kenworthy.

The co-chairs for this program had decided that Rose would introduce Ezra Temple and Ellie would thank all for attending when it was over.

Rose went to the center aisle from her place at the side aisle seat on the front row. As she briefly scanned the audience and all those unfamiliar faces, she asked for help from a Higher Power to get through this without fainting. She did feel a little weak in the knees. The words flowed as if she were guided not by her written notes but by her seventh grade Sunday school teacher at St. James the Lesser Episcopal Church in New Haven, Connecticut. Mrs. Endicott had no idea of the impact she had on young Rose Beckham as she prepared her to join the church and take solemn vows to live for Jesus Christ. She had passed the test before; could she do it now?

Chapter Twenty-Eight

A Bad News Phone Call
March 21, 1935

Fred Trotman paced about his office wondering about what Ellie and Rose had done? Ever since that night when they began to plan for the symphony orchestra for Fort Anthony, Ezra Temple had been a thorn in his side. Fred was aware of the latent presence of the Klan in this area. Members and lapsed members held onto the same beliefs and political ambitions prevalent ten years ago. The size of his student body was one of his most important responsibilities, and they could boycott the school at any time. The Kleagle could march on the campus or burn a cross or burn a building. This could be a mess and I would be the big loser!

Fred admitted to himself that Professor Temple was not at fault. He was there at the reception as his guest in order to show the city leadership that he was supportive of the arts and particularly music. It is not as if his plan backfired on him but things were a bit out of hand. Rose Beckham Roberts—that Connecticut Yankee—had come in here and had caused all this. She is a serious influence on Ellie and he was not sure it suited his plans. President of this little teachers college in the boondocks of Indiana was not the end of the road for him. He was not going to allow Rose to foul up his ambitions to head a major university and soon. His time was running out.

The phone rang and he had to answer it himself since Julia had gone to the program at church.

"This is a collect call for Mr. Ezra Temple from his mother," intoned the operator.

"This is not Mr. Temple, but I will accept the charges."

When he completed that call, he made another quick one, grabbed his hat and headed for the church. He arrived as Rose was introducing her guest performers. He stood at the rear to better see and hear the performance. In actuality, he was a distraction to Rose but she completed her introduction and sat comfortable that she would have made Mrs. Endicott proud of her.

She sat down next to Ellie in the second seat since Ellie was to speak after the program.

"Fred is in the back."

"He told me at breakfast that he wasn't coming."

"I guess he changed his mind."

Soon Randy Roberts joined him at the rear of the Sanctuary.

"What's goin'on for Gods sake?"

"I'll tell you when this is over. Relax its okay."

The program included Negro spirituals, Baptist blood hymns and Methodist standards.

Ezra Temple had arranged each one to fit the voices he had to work with since he found his Travelers were very versatile. Some real talent he had assembled for this his first public performance in Fort Anthony since the party.

The small group was assembled on the podium and the kneeling platform in front of the altar rail, which was opened for this purpose. Ezra carefully placed himself in the center of the middle aisle about five feet back from the first rank of singers. He did not use a music stand and had no hymnals or music folders to distract from their performance. The Preacher had a small spinet moved into the space to Ezra's left and Ladye Frances Hayes, Bishops Hayes daughter, was seated on the padded bench.

He did not say a word heard by anyone in the audience. Their faces lit up when he addressed his singers with just the movement of his lips.

Ezra raised his left hand slowly as if pointing to his bass and baritone.

"Steal away, steal away"

Then to the tenor . . . "Steal away home"

As one voice they all sang in hushed tones;

"I ain't got long to stay here.

My Lord He calls me, He calls me by the trumpet;

The trumpet sounds within a my soul,

I ain't got long to stay here."

Each verse was more dramatic than the last. The audience was stunned at the accapella performance of the little group of believers from The New Awakenings Baptist Church. However, they sat on their hands.

Bishop Kenworthy stood quietly and said "Amen"; others said "Praise God" or "Praise the Lord."

Fred Trotman was moved to applaud. Methodists did not applaud the singing of a sacred song in the sanctuary of the First Methodist Church of Fort Anthony, Indiana. It had been rumored that Fred was a Baptist before he came to lead the Teachers College.

It was the first day of spring; some buds were on the dogwood, and the redbuds were almost in flower. The warming sun was brightly glowing through the leaded glass windows. Each color-filled window on the east side of the sanctuary seemed to cry out in the glory of the moment!

The program was almost over when the Bishop asked Ezra if the group would sing the last three verses of the hymn with which he had begun the service. He went to the choir loft, selected an armful of Methodist Hymnals, and announced to the assembled group this change in plan. They all scuffled around to find the words in the hymnal so they could be part of this moving experience.

Ezra announced that the last number performed by the choir would be "Roll Jordan Roll." He thanked the dignitaries who had come and particularly President Fred Trotman who had made it possible for him to be here in Fort Anthony and for his strong support of the music program at the school.

He again raised his left hand pointing to Ladye Frances who began to play softly. The organist at the large pipe organ joined in and the choir in perfect four-part harmony began the words.

The entire audience stood as the little group went rolling down the Jordan led by Ezra Nehemiah Temple.

The program ended as it had begun with the audience singing the power filled words of this radical hymn.

In Him shall true hearts everywhere
Their high communion find
His service is the golden cord
Close binding all mankind.

Join hands, then brothers of the faith,
What'eer your race may be
Who serves my Father as a son
Is surely kin to me.

In Christ now meet both east and west,
In Him, meet south and north
All Christly souls are one in Him
Throughout the whole wide earth.

Bishop Kenworthy gave the Benediction.

As the crowd began to file out joyously, Ellie said; "Well, I got off light."

"Aren't you glad?"

"Sure am."

The two women went over to the guest performers to invite them to lunch. The two men begged off but the ladies said, yes, they had planned to stay.

They both finally made their way to Ez who was engaged in his conversation with the Bishops and Fred Trotman.

Bishop Kenworthy said, "Fred, I know you are pleased to have such a talented arranger/conductor on your music school staff." Bishop Hayes asked, "Would it be possible for an older person such as me to attend some classes? Regrettably, I have not finished school. Brother Trotman, do you think it is too late?"

"Bishop, it is never too late to expand your mind and your horizons. I would suggest that you audit a course or two and decide for yourself. Come by my office soon and I will introduce you to some classes we offer that should be interesting to you."

The ladies waited patiently for their hero to join them for the walk down to the fellowship hall and lunch.

As they entered the room, everyone rose and even the most staid of old Methodists joined in an ovation for the young colored man. As they finished lunch, Fred came over to the head table and asked to speak to Ez privately.

CHAPTER TWENTY-NINE

Calling in the Big Guns
Thursday Afternoon, March 21, 1935

President Fred Trotman had good connections to the Governor of Indiana so when he called his office for a favor it was honored.

A highway patrolman met Ez at his house on Hardscuffle Road with orders to get him to Saint Joseph Hospital in Lexington, Kentucky with all due haste. Suddenly, Ezra Temple had become a star in Fort Anthony. His friends, neighbors and fans there, met the news of his father's stroke and imminent death with shock and sadness.

Ezra did not know anything except what Fred Trotman had been able to convey from the brief conversation with Esther. He told Esther he would get him there in a hurry and he did his best to honor that commitment.

Job Temple had always been a hard working man who put his work and family ahead of his own health. Ezra knew the doctors had him on digitalis and other drugs for his heart and high blood pressure but he did not realize that Job was in danger.

Ezra prayed for God to bring him back to full health. He prayed for his mother, too that she might have the strength to cope with this difficult situation. They had been married for so long and Ester was devoted to Job and dependent on him as well.

She taught school but Job was the strong force in the family. He was a Christian, a man of color, and a responsible citizen. His father had always reminded him of his obligation to country and Abraham Lincoln. Job joined the U.S. Army as a child of the South but who appreciated the Union and what it had meant to persons of color. He told Ezra that saving the Union was the greatest thing Lincoln ever did and if the time came for him to stand with it, he should do it. He never mentioned the Proclamation as they called it but in the context of Lincoln and the Republican Party. All these things were irrelevant to Ezra but his mind was full of memories of his dad. He was so glad that Job had been with him to go to the funeral of Lilah and then on to Nashville to meet his old friend W.O.Palmer.

Tears came as he thought of the possibility that his dad might not see him complete his education. He became more determined than ever to reach beyond his grasp.

But he was tired. The program at the Methodist church was a lot of fulfilling work. At the first stop, he asked the trooper if he could lie down in the back seat. The sounds of the tires on asphalt for mile upon mile set him sound asleep. He woke up at a stoplight in Indianapolis and asked if they could stop so he could use the restroom. He bought a Dr. Pepper and some crackers for himself and the trooper. The trooper stopped in New Albany at the state garage to fill up with gas and check with headquarters. Fred Trotman had called his boss to tell him that Job Temple was holding his own but please ask the trooper to move with all due haste to safely transport his friend to the St. Joseph Hospital in Lexington. The trooper did not know who Ezra was but he knew that this trip was being made at the direct order of the Governor. He contacted the Kentucky State Police and asked for speedy passage down the highway to Lexington. In every town between Louisville and Lexington, he received a courtesy escort through every red light all the way.

When they came into Lexington, the escort led them directly

to the entry of the hospital. Esther was waiting with little Ezra and ZD Eakerly.

Esther was weeping but said, "He is still with us."

ZD took him by the arm and promptly took him to the room where his father lay in an oxygen tent, his life slowly slipping away.

Chapter Thirty

Another Funeral
Sunday Afternoon, March 24, 1935

The memorial service was held at the chapel on the campus of Eastern Kentucky Agriculture School. Dr. Eakerly gave a eulogy and Ezra offered a reflection on his father and the sad journey they had recently made to bury his young wife. He described his father as a rock of friendship, support, the joy and purpose of his life.

The campus Chaplain conducted the non-denominational service. Job had been cremated in Lexington according to his wishes. Esther had the ashes placed in a bronze urn and she took them with her.

She told Ezra that although she did not know where or when she might meet her Maker she wished to be cremated and her ashes mingled with Job and placed in a capsule for disposal wherever he pleased. This made the entire affair difficult for Ezra but he understood and intended to carry out her wishes perfectly.

The discussion of her future and that of Little Ezra was easy for Esther to work out in her mind.

"But I want you to come back to Fort Anthony with me. We could live together, or if you like I will arrange for separate quarters for you."

"Why can't I keep Little Ezra with me? It will be easier for me and he is making splendid progress at school."

"At school?" Ez said "Momma, what is he doing at school."

"I take him with me when I go. He is a hit with the other teachers who are tutoring him. He is learning to read and write."

"But Momma, he is just four years old!"

She continued, "he spells and plays the sweet potato and some xylophone. Furthermore, he is almost five. His birthday is next month. Have you been away so long that you have forgotten?"

"This is unforgivable of me. April 17th is it not?"

"Yes, and we will need to celebrate soon!"

"Who is teaching him music?"

"The same somebody who taught you music. Your Momma."

"But I didn't start till I was six."

"He is smarter than you were."

"Momma, you are wonderful."

"I do the best I can."

"Momma, you are the best."

"Alright," he said, "how about this: You stay here until the end of school."

"And take care of Little Ezra?"

"I'll take your application back if you want to teach up there and you and Easy can come up this summer. I can fix up the house or find a better place and we can find somebody to keep Little Ezra while you aren't there."

"And have somebody else raise this child? Not on your life."

"But, I plan to begin at I.U. right away."

"I'll stay here with your son, I'll continue to take him to school with me and teach him the same things all my first graders are learning.

"If I can start taking classes this summer I'll get a head start on my Masters," he said, having not thought it through completely.

She wisely replied, "I'll continue helping him with his music and we will come up there when he is ready for the first grade. That will be in September of '36. Whatcha think?"

"I think I know what my Master's Thesis can be and I can do it pretty quickly. I'll be on my way by the time the two of you get there next year." They continued to make plans for the boy in an animated manner but she knew that he was biting off a lot. He would learn.

Esther gave the Model T Truck back to the school in much better shape than when Job took it over a few months ago. ZD agreed with the plans and encouraged Esther to stay in the little house on the campus for one dollar per month. He would have some coal sent down when he received a load and the school would pick up the little light bill. Ezra encouraged her to get a telephone. He would feel that they were much more secure if they could call up to ZD's house in case of trouble.

The trooper was long gone back to Indiana so ZD suggested that Ez drive the panel truck back to school.

He was on a new road but could not know where it ended.

Chapter Thirty-One

Visit to Bloomington
Tuesday, March 26, 1935

Ez stopped at Bloomington on Monday night as he slowly made his way back to Western Indiana State. He slept in the back of the panel truck on some of his dad's clothes that Esther insisted he take with him. He felt strange but he was warmed on this cool spring night by his memories of his father and his big black overcoat. He awoke in the parking lot of the gymnasium and walked in to the men's locker room where he relieved himself and took a shower and shaved. He put on the suit he had worn to the funeral and went to the cafeteria for some breakfast. He still had six dollars on him and the breakfast was 15 cents plus 5 cents for coffee. He was prepared for the day.

He left the truck parked in the gym lot and headed towards the Music School. The dean had not come in yet but the receptionist said it would be okay to look around. He was impressed. The school had a small library, practice rooms, a recital hall and a few classrooms. On the walls were photos of performers who had appeared in concert.

Presently, the receptionist asked if the Dean was expecting him.

"This is a drop in and I hoped I could catch him in his office."

"He won't be in until ten. Could someone else help?"

"I plan to enroll here as soon as possible and I need some help with that."

"Let me call Dr. McDonald. Perhaps she could help."

"That will be fine."

She appeared with a clipboard, looking every bit the efficient school-marm in a double-breasted chalk striped banker's suit, white shirt, striped tie, cuffed pants and all.

"May I help you, young man?"

"I hope so. I would like to enroll here at I.U. to work on my Master's."

"Whoa! Hold on here. What is your name?"

"I'm sorry. I did not introduce myself. My name is Ezra Nehemiah Temple."

"Where did you get your Bachelor's Degree?"

"My undergraduate degree is from Eastern Kentucky Agricultural School."

"What is your current occupation?"

"I am on the faculty at the Teachers College in Fort Anthony, Indiana. My friend Dr. W.O.Palmer recommended your school to me and Dr. Trotman called Dr. Willson who said that it would be okay for me to come down here to school."

"You mean Dr. Willson the President of the University?"

"Yes, I believe so."

"Well, I don't recall that he told me that. He thinks every Negro boy who can whistle 'Dixie' and walk at the same time is a candidate for my music school."

"Would you check with his office, please ma'am?"

"Please stop referring to me as ma'am. My name is Dr. Helen McDonald, MA, Ph.D.and I am in charge of admissions here and you should refer to me as Dr. McDonald. I am not Mrs. McDonald, I am not Miss McDonald, and I am not Madame McDonald, which I assume is the appellation, which you and those like you have shortened to 'Ma'am!'"

"Dr. McDonald, I beg your pardon, but it is my long held belief, supported by my study of the parochial dialects of the South, that it is not clear if your premise is correct. Perhaps, 'Ma'am' refers to the mammary glands upon which we all receive a good start on life. In any case, I will be happy to refer to you as Dr. McDonald in the future."

"Let us begin once more if you please. Dr. McDonald, would you please check with Dr. Willson's office about my status here at Indiana University? I would like to begin the process of matriculation at the earliest possible moment in time."

She turned and went to the receptionist desk.

He bit his lip. He thought, "Boy you are in deep trouble. What a smartass you are. I have to apologize and quickly!"

"Er, Dr. McDonald—"

"Yes, Mr.-ah, what did you say your name is?"

He was tempted to run out the door and start over again with his life. What a stupid thing to do. He was tired and sooo weary of people dying, of riding back and forth on narrow country roads in the dark, of sleeping in the back of an old panel truck. He was feeling sorry for himself and suddenly began to cry. He went outside and sat on the cut limestone steps leading up to the entrance. He felt like he was falling apart. "Get yourself together boy, this is the first day of a new life for you. Take it easy. Cry it out. You deserve it." After about an hour, he was able to get up and walk around the campus a bit. He took a seat on a park bench under a small shelter. A little shower came up and he was glad for the solitude.

In a moment, an umbrella poking him on the leg disturbed him.

"Hey, man, what's going on with you?"

"Just resting, I'm a little tired."

"They sent me looking for you."

"Who are you?"

"I'm Barry, a student at the Music School."

"Who's they?"

"The folks over at the music school. You are Ezra Temple aren't you?"

"I was. I'm not sure who I am right now."

"Hey, man I know how you feel. That bitch can castrate a man in a New York second."

"What's her act?"

"Oh, she's the local dike who can't get a job nowhere else and the Dean said he would take her on. C'mon, he's waiting on you!"

Ez yawned a few times took ten deep breaths and said, "Okay, I'm ready to face the 'music' so to speak."

Ezra began to think about the gravity of the situation. For years, he did not have much direction in his life. Playing music was enough. Now, thanks to his folks, Dr. Eakerly, Bishop Hayes, Dr. Trotman and all the nice people in Ft. Anthony he was on his way, to where remained a mystery.

The Associate Dean of the School and band director, Sam Goodrich, was a trumpet player who had been on the road most of his life. He had been in Sousa's band, played with the Army Band out of Fort Meade when Calvin Coolidge was President, received his Masters in Public Administration from George Washington when he was in D.C. and had retired with 30 years and came to IU to help save a struggling music school. From First Sergeant to Interim Dean of a Music School was not a lateral move but he didn't mind the step down. He had his retirement pay and even though the salaries in Higher Ed were not much, he got along fine.

"Come in Professor Temple. I apologize for Dr. McDonald's abrupt behavior. She is a good person though a little overly protective of me. I would not do what she does and President Wilson did not think she could do what he wanted me to do, so here I am and there she is—glad to see you."

"I am very pleased to be here."

I see by your resume you play jazz clarinet. And W.O. says a good one.

"Yessir."

"Perhaps you would like to join our little group for our Sunday afternoon sessions. Sometimes we have an audience. I think you would enjoy the setup. We play in the round and the performances are known on campus as 'Session at the Circle.'"

"Sounds fascinating; you have talked to Dr. Palmer?"

"Well, we deans do visit back and forth between official meetings of our national associations. He says he is a friend of your dad."

"Was a friend. Dad died last week."

"Good God, son I heard that your wife had died giving birth recently but I did not hear about your father."

"Dr. Palmer does not know either. I should write him. Things have been a little confusing lately and I had just completed doing a program for some of the ladies in Fort Anthony when I heard about his stroke. They got me down there in a hurry but I just barely saw him take his last breath. I'll miss him."

"Would you like to call Bill from my conference room?"

"That's very thoughtful of you."

"I know how impressed he was with you and he spoke highly of your dad. Go on, here is his number. Dial it straight through. No PBX operator on that phone."

Chapter Thirty-Two

Easy
Tuesday Morning, March 26, 1935

"Will Mama be back soon, Granny?"

"Not soon, sonny. She is with God in Heaven."

"Does she know Jesus, Granny?"

"Oh, I hope so, don't you?"

"Yes'm. Do you know Jesus, Granny?"

"I meet Him every day. I see Him in your bright face. I see Him in Uncle ZD. I see Him when I think about your grandpa; I see Him when I think about your Daddy."

"Will daddy be back soon, Granny?"

"Well, maybe not soon, but he will be back."

"Do you love me, Granny?"

"More than life itself, chile!"

"I love you, Granny. Are you going to heaven to be with Jesus soon, Granny?"

"I am with Jesus when I am with you. I don't want to leave you, ever."

"Thanks, granny. I don't want to leave you either. I really love you, Granny."

"Thanks, sonny, now let's go to school."

"Granny, why do you call me sonny?"

"Well, how about E Z?"

"You mean like Easy?"

"Yes'm, I like that."

"I like that too."

"Come on Easy, let's go to school."

"Yes'm. Let's go."

She wished that Lilah, Job, and Ez had been here. She would wish that a thousand times in the next few years. He is bright, she thought. I think I'll have him tested next month.

It was with considerable joy when she wrote Ez and shared her conversation with Easy Temple. "He is a lovely and lovable little boy," she wrote.

Chapter Thirty-Three

The Preacher Calls
Tuesday Morning, March 26, 1935

"Randy, this is Vern. Can I come by to see you sometime soon?"

"How about lunch?"

"11:45?"

"Fine, see you at the tea room?"

"My treat."

"Deal."

Ever since Bishop Kenworthy had visited town Vern had been like a worm in hot ashes. He had ideas for this or that betterment project for the city. However, Randy was not ready for the bombshell about to be dropped.

After some small talk and a brief prayer by the preacher over the food, Randy asked, "What's on your mind, Vern?"

"Our city is among the most forward looking in the state and it is largely because of your youth, your upbringing, and your world view that stems from a wonderful education at Yale."

"Oh my God," Randy thought "he's setting me up for something big."

"When Ed Kenworthy was in town last week, he went over to what some call 'Nigger Hill' to pick up Bishop Hayes.

"Who doesn't call it that?"

"That's beside the point. Afterwards he expressed concern that those folks lived in something akin to a slum and he told me that our city was better than that."

"Hardscuffle is a county road. It is not in the city!"

"I went over myself and even walked around some with Bishop Hayes to visit some of his parishioners."

"The phrase 'even walked around' is condescending, Preacher!"

"Are you going to listen to me or do I need to talk to Rose first?"

"Vern, if we were not in public, the Mayor and Bank President, I would slap hell out of you for that remark."

"I apologize. Could I continue?"

"Yeah, but leave out the piosity and references to my married life. Rose and I are a team. She saves my butt in a lot ways. I could not do as well as I do without her. Now what do you want?"

"We prayed with the infirm; we joked with some of the elders; we had tea with some of the deaconesses and I promised God in heaven that I would talk to you about it."

"Terrific", Randy thought. "And?"

"Well, you need to do something about it."

"Me?"

Vern was insistent, "You are the Mayor; you are the Chairman and President of our biggest bank. Frankly, I think you may want to be Governor or Senator from Indiana one of these days. You are a Republican and most of these coloreds who have come up from Tennessee, Alabama, and other parts of the South are Republicans as well. I am not the one to be giving you political advice. I am apolitical or try to be, but you can change this situation and we will all be better off!"

Randy responded to this argument, "Nigger Hill as it is called by some is not even within the city limits. If we try to extend the city limits we will have to extend our city services over there, they will have to pay city taxes, the city will have to sell a lot of municipal bonds and doubtless raise taxes on property now in the city. I'll be burned at the stake in front of City Hall if I try that."

"Tell you what I'll do. I'll preach a series on the subject of the Good Samaritan. I'll explain what the radical Christ was talking about when he shook up all those folks 2,000 years ago. I'll explain that the folks on Nigger Hill are our neighbors even though they are not inside the city limits of Fort Anthony. I will repeat Bishop Hayes comments about Uncle Ezra and his prayer for all the children even unto the last generation. I will publicly urge the City Fathers to do something about the slums just outside the city limits. In other words, I will help you, I will give you some cover, I will get as many of my colleagues in other pulpits briefed and preaching on the same topic about the same time. I will do my part. Will you do yours?"

"Holy cow, Vern, that's blackmail!"

"No Randy, it's the Gospel. Would you pass the rolls?

Randolph Roberts went home that night and poured himself a double hit of Scotch. He looked straight at Rose and said, "That sonuvabuck."

"Who, honey?"

"That dang preacher of ours."

"You shouldn't talk about Vern Shipley like that! What's he done now, for goodness sakes?"

"He's on some kind of reform kick and now he wants the city to annex Nigger Hill and extend city services out there."

"Well, it is not a very pleasant place to live and bring up little children. They don't have running water, most of them don't have electricity, no sidewalks, the road is a big rock pile and the school that the county provides for them is pitiful. I think that's a good idea."

Randy thought to himself, "Why did Fred Trotman ever invite Ez

Temple to that reception about the symphony?"

"Well, we can't do all that and help fund a symphony orchestra as well. And where is the money going to come from to pay for it?"

"Call your Senator friend and tell him you want some of that Roosevelt money from that emergency relief bunch, a big CCC work crew and the CWA to help out."

"To hell with FDR. It is our money. Quit calling it 'Roosevelt' money."

"Sweetheart, I won't call it Roosevelt money if you will call Senator Roundtree."

Ed Roundtree was a staunch Republican who hated Franklin Roosevelt. He told the State Bankers Convention once that Roosevelt was going to break the Nation. Cordell Hull had asked enough to chew on with his Good Neighbor Policy in our own hemisphere.

"Senator Roundtree, please."

"Mayor Randolph Roberts."

"Yes, I'll wait."

"Thanks, would you ask him to call me in Fort Anthony—Main 6046." "Yes, my office at the bank, thanks again."

Randy knew that his members of Congress were loaded with calls like his, but this was a good project and deserved some help. Roosevelt had tasked Harry Hopkins, a former social worker, to lead the Federal Emergency Relief Administration (FERA). This agency sent funds to aid local relief agencies. Within two hours, Hopkins gave away five million dollars. He believed that men should be put to work and not be given charity so his program also funded public work programs through new agencies like the CWA (Civil Works Administration). Its public works program gave the unemployed jobs building or repairing roads, parks, airports, etc. The most famous was the (CCC) Civilian Conservation Corps. This put 2.5 million unmarried men to work maintaining and restoring forests, beaches, and parks. Workers earned only $1 a day but received free room and board and job training. The young men of America were taught how to live independently, thus, increasing their self-esteem.

"Vern, Randy—"

"I'm doing fine. Talked to Ed Roundtree and he will help get some U. S. Government support and some of the money we send to the Federal Government sent back to us to upgrade some parts of our city. We still have the problem of annexation. I need your help on that."

Vern said, "Of course, I will do what I can."

Randy thought, "You sneaky bastard you better help all you can." "I'll do everything a small town mayor can do to get the money; you get somebody on the council to front the annexation."

Vern made a suggestion, "How about Louise Edwards?"

"Jeeminny, that is a stroke of genius. She wants to be the next Mayor and if she is able to pull this off, she deserves it. I'll be glad to let her have it."

In Fort Anthony the members of the council passed the job of Mayor around and Randy's term was about up. He didn't need this kind of trouble for himself or the bank.

Chapter Thirty-Four

On The Way Back To School
Tuesday Afternoon, March 26, 1935

Ez had mixed feelings about his situation. He realized that he had made commitments to IU, to Western Indiana State Teachers College, to the church, to his momma and his son! He must soon work out a schedule to meet all those and others he would make. He began to prioritize his obligations:

1. Momma and little Ez
2. Northwest Indiana State Teachers College
3. The New Awakenings Baptist Church

"No," he thought, "ZD will be there for Momma and Momma will be there for Little Ez."

1. IU
2. WISTC
3. Church

He thought to himself "Ladye Frances is experienced enough to cover for me, but I have to watch our schedule to coordinate my other stuff with the church. I'll talk to Uncle Hannibal. He wants me to finish my education first, I'm sure of that."

"Let's see. . .I better talk to Trotman. He'll help me on this one for sure."

When he was on the campus, he headed the truck to the Ad Building to see President Trotman. He needed to report and thank him for all the trouble he went to for him.

"Come in, Ez:" Fred Trotman was as gracious as he could be. "I'm sorry about your dad. He must have been a fine man."

"Thank you; he was a special person."

"Bishop Hayes told us about him, his research work and the job that he did at Eastern Kentucky Agricultural School. How are your mom and little boy?"

"Thank you. They are good. I admired my father very much and we had many good times together. He taught me to love 'God's Only Earth' as he called it. He was the best husband a woman could find and I wish I could have been such a man."

"You are a good man, Ez, and he was surely proud of you and what you are about to do. You are taking on quite a load you know."

"I am aware of that and I have been giving a lot of thought to it."

"Your life will be enriched and you will be an inspiration to thousands of other people during you career because of your decision to continue your formal education and get your masters degree."

"I hope so."

"What are your immediate plans?"

"Can we talk some about that? I want your advice as to how I can meet my obligations to our school and to the program at IU."

"You know we want to cooperate in every way."

"I stopped to see the Dean and he is enthusiastic about my involvement in his program. What did you tell them about me?"

"Plenty," he said with a twinkle in his eye and his mouth cocked to his left.

"You must have been very generous."

"We gave you a good recommendation and sent an updated CV based on what we know about you since you first applied here. Only the facts, Professor."

"I am grateful to you for so many things. The ride to Richmond made me feel like I was somebody and the trooper was very helpful. I need to write him and the Governors office."

Trotman jumped in, "You write the trooper. I'll take care of the Governors office!" Fred thought, "Sometimes the written word is better left unwritten!"

Chapter Thirty-Five

Gathering of Some Pilgrims
Thursday Morning, March 28, 1935

Almost all of the clergy of Fort Anthony and some lay leaders were gathered in the large conference room of the First Methodist Church. Vern had called them together. They shared coffee and a roll and left as Vern had planned at 10:30 on this Thursday morning in March. It was cool but the sun was shining and the group was in a good spirits although the school bus was not very comfortable. A few of the more obese of the lay members of the group had a very hard time fitting themselves into the seats at all. Vern had not told them where but he had promised them an interesting tour.

The membership at the Methodist Church was double the size of the next largest congregation. To preachers, quantity is number one priority. More members to give more money, more money bigger salary (but not much), bigger salary happier wife, happier wife better sermons, better sermons more members, etc. He must have a happy wife and preach some hellacious sermon.

Vern stood at the front and shouted toward the rear of the bus, "I hope this short tour will be enlightening to some of you and a time of re–acquaintance for others. We are going up Hardscuffle Road and will be welcomed by my friend and our Brother in Christ, Hannibal Hayes. Afterward we will take a walking tour of the neighborhood, and toward the end, we will visit the park for a luncheon and a discussion. We will be there shortly."

Vern took his seat and a low murmur was evident among the riders of the bus. Most sat quietly. Vern was nervous, as well he should have been. All of the congregations were segregated and some had members who were more active in the Ku Klux Klan than in the church.

One clergyman from such a church said, "Shipley, this is a setup! Stop the bus I want off now!"

Vern had expected this and said, "Sure, Red, Anyone else who wants to get off?

Jim Bartley said, "Aw, sit down Red. You might learn something."

"I don't need to learn a dang thing from some nigger preacher! Stop this bus now!"

The larger man next to Red was a member of his church said quietly, "Sit down Red." He did.

Vern sat quietly as well and let the matter run its course. The short drive up Hardscuffle Road shook the school bus badly. Soon the bus pulled up in front of the New Awakenings Baptist Church of Nigger Hill and the assorted group of Christians filed off and into the little building.

Bishop Hayes greeted them and six of the twelve members of the New Awakenings Travelers welcomed them with their new theme: "In Christ there is no East or West." Ez was not present, and Ladye Frances Hayes accompanied them on the old upright piano. The organ is their pride and joy, and no one except Ez Temple was allowed to touch it.

Vern stood and told of his interest here today. In his most reserved and politic manner he explained a few things:

1. This neighborhood is in the county.
2. This neighborhood is adjacent to our city.
3. This neighborhood is where most of our domestic help lives.
4. This neighborhood does not have modern services.

Some call this neighborhood a slum and no place to raise children!

"At our house we love our cook, our maid and at the church we love all those people who across the years have served the cause of Christ through their work at the First Methodist Church of Fort Anthony. We love them as Christ loves us and as friends in our homes. I sometimes think that Anna loves Mamie more than me. And for good reason, I suppose. I cannot continue to let this carbuncle on the backside of our city fester and grow and cause so much pain for so many. I have redirected my ambitions for ministry. My ambition is to make this place we call home a neighborhood where we love one another, bind up the wounds of our neighbors, and make our entire community a place where if Christ were to come here tomorrow He could say 'well done, good and faithful people'. While many of us have 'faith' in many things, I have 'faith' that the Love of Christ as a way of life will work in my life and in yours. That may be too simple for many of you but I must admit my faith is simple. That is too simple for my own faith community, but it is my personal belief. This is the new, radical Vern Shipley speaking."

"What's this going to cost us?"

"Who's going to pay for it?"

"When are you going to start?"

"Will this be a city or a county project?"

"We're in the middle of a depression. This is not a good time."

Vern satisfactorily answered most the queries but asked them to hold their questions for a while.

"I recall a story that Hannibal Hayes told recently in our sanctuary about Old Uncle Ezra. Today before we take a little walk on the road up "Nigger Hill" I want my Brother to tell that story and offer a prayer."

The Bishop retold the story of the Ezra he had known in his growing up church in Alabama. How Uncle Ezra, as everyone called him, always prayed for the children. "I suppose he thought accordingly that our only hope was in our children. Uncle Ezra prayed for the children here today, for those we are expecting soon and all those children of the future, those children who would people this earth for all the millennia ahead until the Lord returns."

He then delivered a brief prayer for all the children of God who were here today and those who might be around when Christ came again.

Chapter Thirty-Six

Concern for the Widow and the Orphan
Saturday, March 30, 1935

"Dr. Eakerly, me and Vashti, have been talking about Miss Esther and little Ezra."

"What about, Early?"

"Just about how they gonna do down there by they selves, without Mr. Job to look after them."

"Are you concerned about their safety?"

"Naw sir, but we are concerned they will be lonely and we thought we would like to have them up here for supper sometimes. We can eat back in the kitchen after you and Miz Rebecca gets done with your evening meal. We thought we could share with them. There is always plenty left."

"Feel welcome to, Early, anytime. Fact is Miss Rebecca and I would like to have them up as our guests occasionally. We get lonely sometimes as well. Ask her to come in please."

"Vashti, Early said that perhaps you would like to have Esther and Little Ezra up for a meal sometime. That is a good idea. We all get lonely every now and then. I will speak to Miss Rebecca and we might like to do that as well. And Early, Little Ezra could use the influence of a good man in his life sometimes. You might want take him fishing this spring or he might be good help in the kitchen garden."

"You reckon Miz Esther would mind?"

"On the contrary, I am sure she would be very pleased."

"I'll do that, too, Dr. Eakerly. Thank you for the suggestion. You ever go fishing, sir?"

"Not in a long time."

"Why don't we both take him, sir?"

"Good idea. As they used to say around home, 'you get a line and I'll get a pole, we'll go down to the old fishing hole'. Remember that, Early?"

"Surely do, sir."

"Well, let's go."

"I'll ask my brother Tan where they are biting."

Chapter Thirty-Seven

Vern Writes Mayor Roberts to Report
Tuesday, April 2, 1935

April 2, 1935

Dear Mayor Roberts:

I recently met with twenty clergy and lay from several of our local congregations and took them for a tour of the colored neighborhood over on the hill. We stopped at the Baptist Church and took a walk from there to the grove that we hope will become known as "Pleasant Hill Park" for some lunch.

The alley they call "Hard Scuffle Road" is, as you know, the main road through the neighborhood. That day the boulders stood six inches up from the surface, mud holes were equally deep and it was indeed a hard scuffle for our white brethren. The county has spread some chert but that has all been washed off into the ditch on the side.

Many of them had never been all the way to the top. I confess I had not. The 'park' sits at the top of the ridge with a beautiful view of the City. The hillside is eroded with very few trees. The vegetation is mostly wild raspberry bushes, black haws, hackberry and hop hornbeams with a few hedge-apple trees in the mix. The grove is still there because it is the site of an old unmarked cemetery.

Most of the shade would have been under an old, old hackberry tree but it had not leafed out yet. There was no place to sit, no picnic tables, so my guests pulled up the deteriorating butt log of a fallen red maple and a fallen and half-rotten butternut hickory.

We shared a couple of loaves of bread, some bologna and a few sodas as our communion meal.

We talked a lot about what we had seen and they came up with some good ideas.

If the county will not improve everything and the county is agreeable they should:

- *Annex the neighborhood/city*
- *Pave the "alley" with some kind of surface that will stay put-joint city/county*
- *Clean out the ditches and install a couple of culverts-city/county*
- *Rename it Pleasant Hill Drive and the neighborhood Pleasant Hill-either the city or the county*
- *Put in water lines-city*
- *Put in gas lines-gas company*
- *Fix up the park some-Civilian Conservation Corps (CCC)*
- *Fence in the cemetery and clean up the grounds and the hillside. CCC*

If we have any building codes we would hope the city could find a way to enforce some of them in Pleasant Hill, but only on our good local citizens who own the real estate.

We agreed to support change through our sermons and our outreach committees. I will preach a series on the lessons to be learned from the Good Samaritan Parable and some of them will do so as well. We had a couple of Klan types who resented my effort but I'm sure we have many substantial businessmen and women who have a similar feeling. I think I can handle them.

I wanted to write this so the record would be clear. Call me when you receive this. I will have it hand delivered by J.C. Owens. Looking forward to working with you, I am

Your servant in Christ,

Vern Shipley

Chapter Thirty-Eight

Plans Being Made
Wednesday, April 3, 1935

"Vern, hey, Randy here—I got your briefing paper, good work. By the way where did you learn the names of the trees?"

"A Yale forester!"

"Glad you changed your mind."

"Look, I'm about to call Judge Leach about the Pleasant Hill proposition."

"Yeah, I like the new name. Bishop Hayes came up with it. That's a relief."

"Ah, should we push them or offer to do a joint venture thing? It is a good opportunity and we could do a bang up job with it."

"Yeah, I agree it could be a model. Good idea, I'll call you when I have talked to Leach."

"Judge Leach please. Mayor Roberts. I'll wait."

"Ross, do you have a minute. I'd like to walk over there for a brief visit. Be right there."

"Come in Randy. Still like Mayor-ing?"

"Yeah it's good."

"When do you step down?

In September—"

"This about the Symphony?"

"No, it's about what some folks call 'Nigger Hill.'"

Judge Leach quickly responded, "That's a problem I wish you had! If you had that and I had a feather in my ear, we'd both be tickled! What about it?"

"I'd like to help."

"That place needs all the help we can get. What do you want to do?"

"Oh, maybe a joint venture deal."

The Judge became suspicious.

"How can that happen?"

"We can do a city-county compact. It's really an urban neighborhood outside our corporate limits but it is not like any other you have in Collier County."

"Oh, I have a few un-incorporated villages."

"Yeah, but this is the only 100% colored village you have. The County Court doesn't pay them much attention. You have a few pretty stiff necked folks on your back."

"By God, that's the truth if it was ever told!"

He pulled out Vern Shipley's letter.

Looking puzzled Judge leach asked, "Who started this?"

"Bishop Kenworthy was in town recently and he went up there to pick up Hannibal Hayes and it hit the fan. He put Vern on the hot seat with orders to solve this. I think he called it a 'Divine Opportunity.'"

"You're kidding."

"Well, maybe not directly but in so many words."

"He needs to stay in Indianapolis."

"Well, what do you say? Aren't you a Methodist too?"

"Yeah, in a little country church. We don't like these so called "big city problems" to get mixed up in our theology. You tell Vern Shipley to leave my preacher Jerry Way out of this stuff!"

"Between Rose and Vern, I've got all I can handle. Think about it, won't you?"

"I am almost certain we can get some help from Washington."

"That would be sweet."

In a friendly voice, he said, "Sure. Hey Randy, come back any time. Bring a small problem next time you want to drop in for a minute."

"I wouldn't have this one if the County Court would do its job," Randy chuckled.

It occurred to him as he left Leach's office, "I think I got his attention!"

Chapter Thirty-Nine

The Mayday Musicale
April 5, 1935

Professor Temple spent 150 percent of his time working with his students as he prepared them for the Mayday Musicale. He had 30 students in his choir and a string quartet. Things were shaping up for a dandy deal.

Rose Roberts got her first clue that a blessed-event might have resulted from the Chicago weekend. It had been almost six weeks and no sign that she would start any time soon. She had some other symptoms so she went to see Dr. Weitzman. He speculated that Rose and Randy would have their first child around the middle of November.

She called Randy at the bank and he was as proud as any rooster in the yard. She called Mother Beckham who said she would make plans to come down soon to visit. Father Beckham was ecstatic. He agreed they must come down soon and see the new mother to be. Rose and Mother Beckham immediately began to discuss what they wanted, a boy or girl. Without much debate, they decided on a girl who would look just like Rose did as a newborn--beautiful. Of course, Randy secretly hoped for a boy but did not say so while Father Beckham hoped for the safe deliverance of a grandchild, period.

The Reverend Dr. Vernon Shipley reported to the Bishop of the progress he was making in his first entry into influencing public policy.

He had prepared a full report with the committee and sent a copy to the Mayor, the County Judge and Senator Roundtree. He sent a blind copy to Bishop Kenworthy. The Bishop encouraged him to keep up the good work, and Vern was ready with his series of sermons. He had invited the "group" back to First Methodist for luncheon and a discussion of the draft plan and he gave each one an outline of his messages on Luke 10:25-37. Some of them agreed to go along and preach the subject while others did not wish it to be publicly known they were involved in this kind of mix of politics and religion. Although Red Lott did not come back, his lay associate did and later came to the Methodist church to worship!

Esther and Easy were invited up to have supper with Evelyn and Early. Early asked if Easy would like to go fishing with him and Easy was beside himself. Dr. Eakerly came back to the kitchen to visit a minute and asked if Easy was going to play the piano like his dad.

"Yessir."

"Well, when are you going to start?"

Esther said, "He is just beginning to pick out a few things."

"You mean he can already play something?"

"Yessir, he has learned his notes and plays the 'Sweet Potato' well and the violin and the xylophone pretty good."

"Well, when you get through with your meal, come in here and show Uncle ZD what you can do."

He jumped up but his grandmother sat him down with "He said after you finish your meal, Easy."

He hurried through his food and asked, "May I be to be excused, please?"

"Take your plate and silver to the sink, Easy."

"Yes'm."

"Now wash your hands."

Vashti said, "you two go on in the music room. Early and I will finish cleaning up."

Dr. Eakerly and Rebecca were reading but had placed a cushion on the piano bench for Easy to sit on. He crawled up on the pillow and fingered the keys a bit. He had his mother's long skinny fingers so he could reach a good span. What they heard next shocked them. Esther sat on the bench with him to reassure him and he began a Chopin piece. It was not long but very melodic and sweet.

Chapter Forty

Songs of Praise
Wednesday, April 10, 1935

Wednesday nights at the New Awakenings Baptist Church had become a community activity where the former prayer meeting had become a time of singing praises. The music director had persuaded the preacher to allow him to experiment with a service of song and instrumental music. He invited his students from the school to join in, and they did. One night a steel guitar player from Tennessee sat in and then a drummer to pick up the beat on some songs joined in.

Soon some of the ladies who had seen the program at the First Methodist Church joined the students—even though some of the husbands felt it might not be safe for women to come over to "Pleasant Hill" at night. The church was filled many Wednesday nights.

One night a famous colored gospel group from Nashville on their way to play a big church in Chicago called Hannibal Hayes to ask if he knew of a place to stay. Hannibal said, "The Lord will provide." With the promise of food and a warm, dry place to stay, the group agreed to perform.

The church was filled on this beautiful spring night and the "Fairhope Five" brought their unique style of accapella southern gospel to the Midwest. The attendees had never heard anything like it. The men earned their keep that night! They sang for an hour, took up a free-will collection and gathered almost ten dollars. They sang another hour for an audience exhausted from clapping and shouting and praising. A few rolled in the aisle. The white folks had never seen anything like that either. Hannibal placed an offering plate on each side of the exit door and collected another ten-fifty in cash and a check from Rose and Randy Roberts for twenty dollars. They had a ball.

The following day Rose went by to see Ez at school to congratulate him on his work at the church, to express her concern for little Ez and his mother and to encourage him to get The Fairhope Five back to Fort Anthony. She was so moved by this exciting genre and the spirit of Wednesday night service she said history was being made with this new style of church music. Ez was kind not to tell Rose that this is standard fare to colored folk. He accepted the enthusiastic praise and went onto his next class. This lady was very nice but he kept his distance. Remembering the symphony reception, he was not about to be burned again.

Chapter Forty-One

The Transfer
Wednesday, April 17, 1935

The County Court of Collier County, Indiana met in regular session and on the agenda was a proposal made jointly by the County Judge and the City Council of Fort Anthony. The Magistrates were more than happy to transfer the Nigger Hill neighborhood with all its problems to the jurisdiction of the city. The city agreed if the County Court agreed. They did, and the deal was done. The quid pro quo was that the county would join the city in a request for some Roosevelt money to improve the public facilities and that the county workhouse gang would come over whenever the city needed them to clean up the area.

"I think that Senator Roundtree can get us some Federal help and a little money to make the deal work." That was Judge Leach in conversation with the Chairman of the Public Works Committee after the meeting.

"If he can't do it, danged if I'm going to spend any county money on that ridge over there. We haven't collected enough taxes there to hire a deputy to keep the peace and God only knows the Sheriff needs one just for that part of the county!"

Judge Leach was happy with the deal he had made.

The following Wednesday some of the deacons met with the preacher to erect a large cross in front of the New Awakenings Baptist

Church in anticipation of Maundy Thursday, Good Friday and Easter Sunday. On Maundy Thursday they had a foot washing service; on Good Friday evening they had a very mournful communion service much like a wake, and on Easter they had a great celebration and decorated the cross with colorful items.

The Wednesday night service was one of mighty praise music and singing. Ez had a choir of his students and the church members; Ladye Frances was on the piano along with drums and a dobro.

They had a record crowd who were lined around the walls and practically hanging from the rafters. Randy drove Rose over that evening and they were a little late. There was no parking in front of the church so he drove into the backyard. As he and Rose began to walk around the church to enter, a car parked across the street from the church scratched off. Randy ran to the front of the church to see the cross burst into flames.

He shouted back to Rose, "Get back in the car!"

He ran around in front in time to hear shots and see a fuel can explode at the front left corner of the church. He burst inside to hear music that was so joyous they could not hear him shout "Get out, get out! The church's on fire!" Unable to capture the attention of the spirited worshipers he began to shout. "Fire, fire, fire, fire!" "Get out quickly folks! Please! The church is on fire!"

Panic followed. Men broke out windows with folding chairs. The back doors, which were ordinarily barricaded, were impossible to break down. The front entry was the only exit– except the low, full height windows.

Randy ran to Ez. "Get out, Ez; you can't save it! Make sure the old folks and the children are okay!" Ez and two of his students were lifting the organ to get it through the crowd to save it. Randy, the affluent banker could not imagine why anyone would attempt to save an old organ when flesh and blood people were in great danger. On the other hand, EZ could not think about not saving this important part of the legacy of the little church!

"Dammit, Ez, put it down. We can replace the organ but we can't replace you!" Ez dropped the old organ and took the arm of a sobbing old colored lady and a lost and screaming white child to guide them to safety. The two students were still struggling with the treasured organ when Ez came back from clearing the sanctuary. A scary cracking sound indicated the ceiling was afire and would soon fall trapping them in the flames and would surely die! They struggled more until Randy appeared again. He grabbed Ez, dragged him out the nearest window and fell to the ground on the left side of the church where the fire was raging in the dry grass. The two students ran out onto Hardscuffle Road and stumbled on the rocks. One broke an ankle, and the other cracked his head on a large stone.

The arsonists had poured fuel on the unpainted clapboard on the side of the church opposite from where Randy and Rose had driven into the backyard. Ez was on fire! Randy had rolled on the ground and put out the burning coat on his back.

Randy prayed, "Not Ez, God, Not Ez, please not Ez, God please, please, please not Ez!" He rushed to him and covered his body with his own, forced him to roll in the grass and extinguish the flames. The other men were pulling women and children from the flaming church and Hannibal Caesar Hayes was on his knees in the middle of Hardscuffle Road praying.

Randy ran around the building to check on Rose. The car was still there, but Rose was nowhere to be found. He went around the backside and she was with Ez praying with him for the little children. "I'm gonna bring your car around here and you take Ez to the hospital." "I'll get those with cars to help load up the other injured and be right behind you." On her way out of the yard, Ez asked her to stop and load the two injured students into the rumble seat.

The church was burned to the ground. The injured and burn victims were transported in cars and wagons. The county had no fire department and there was no volunteer fire department to serve the homes and buildings on Hardscuffle Road. All were saved; 40 were injured most with burns and bruises.

The Lord was with the folks at the New Awakenings Baptist Church on Wednesday night before Easter 1935 and they praised Him for His mercy.

Chapter Forty-Two

The Governor Visits
Wednesday Night, April 17, 1935

Vern Shipley met them at the hospital to help in some small way if he could. He felt guilty since he had been so forward about making improvements to the colored neighborhood. It was he, who, after all, had invited some of his clergy colleagues to visit that largely ignored place. He described it as a carbuncle on the backside of Fort Anthony. It was he who put the heat on Mayor Roberts, a church member. It was his church member Mayor Roberts who in turn leaned on Judge Leach. It was he who, well, what could he say, he caused people who might fear colored folks to come out that Wednesday night. This overwhelming feeling of remorse took him to his knees in prayer.

It was in this attitude of prayer that Rose Roberts found him in the waiting room outside the emergency treatment room of the little hospital. It startled Rose and she kneeled down beside him to comfort him as he sobbed into his pocket-handkerchief. She comforted him and began to pray as well. Her husband was being treated as they prayed. Their friend Ez Temple was in serious condition with burns on his back and arms. Little children were crying in pain and mothers were moaning in sorrow and anger.

It was a good twenty minutes before either recovered their composure. Soon the little emergency room was overrun with physicians and nurses from all over. Burn treatment supplies were in short supply and a call went out to Indianapolis and Chicago for more. Broken bones were being set and temporary splints applied by the Scoutmaster who had been a medic in WWI. It was a scene of skilled and unskilled persons doing what they could to alleviate suffering.

Outside the building, a service of prayer and hymns from all the clergy and people assembled was taking place-- a spontaneous affair, beautiful to behold. Rose and Vern walked to a quiet spot where he unloaded his guilt on her. She was dumbfounded!

"My gracious, Vern, you were doing what was best for all of us. Randy wants to help make Fort Anthony a better place and so does Judge Leach. You were doing your job beautifully. When you stop doing your job in the way you feel lead by God through Christ you should fold up your tent and get out of the business. I mean it. We support you and will as long as we feel like you are being true to your call!"

With a wide grin, she blurted, "Now let me tell you something, we are expecting—in November."

"What great news!" He hugged her and pecked her on the cheek. "If it is a little girl I hope she will be just like you. God sent you as an angel to me tonight! You helped me get past a rough spell. We love you and Randy very much and appreciate your support of what we do."

Fred Trotman and Ellie ran up to Vern and Rose "How is Randy?"

Rose said, "He's fine-nothing first degree. He will be okay soon."

"How about Ez, our reports were that he is in pretty bad shape."

Vern spoke "Brother Hayes has been with him and he said he has burns on his back and arms."

"How about his hands?"

"No report of that, thank God."

"Everyone else alive?"

"So far."

A highway patrol car pulled up and Governor Homer Beasley stepped out. "Fred thanks for calling. I got here as soon as I could."

"Who can give me a report? How is the Mayor? Who would do such a thing? I called General Smythe and he will be here with the Guard Military Police unit soon. What else can we do?"

Fred quickly said, "First, let me introduce these folks."

"Mrs. Roberts, I am so sorry about Randy. His family has meant a lot to Indiana and he has that quality of leadership of which his folks can be very proud."

"Thank you, Governor. I will pass that along to him."

"Could I see him, I would like to tell him myself."

"Let's go see."

On the way to see Randy, Rose gave the governor a first hand report on what she had seen.

"Are you saying you saw some men running to their vehicle after Randy went into the church? Who were they?"

"I'm a little frightened to say. I think I saw one of them at church sometime lately."

"No," gulped the Governor. They visited briefly. The Governor was glowing in his talk about Randy's bravery and the work he was doing as Mayor.

Homer Beasley had been raised by parents who were pious members of the Friends Community near Richmond, Indiana. He graduated from Earlham College and went to a Friends mission school in Ramallah, Palestine to teach geography. He learned to love the townspeople, especially a girl who was a graduate of the Friends Girls School and was then studying at The American University in Beirut. After Homer graduated from Yale Law School, he went back and they were married. Zehwa Azzouni had received a graduate degree in International Studies and after they married, she continued to pursue her studies at Georgetown while Homer worked for the Republican Senator from Indiana on Capitol Hill. He had a deep abiding interest in the fair treatment of ethnics and minorities.

Governor Beasley asked Fred Trotman to give his driver directions to the scene.

"Why don't I ride over with you? Ellie would you like to go with us or stay with Rose?"

Ellie stayed with Rose so Fred had the chance to fully brief the Governor on the situation.

"Dangit, Fred this can't be allowed to happen in my state. I won't have a church burning in Indiana. We are going to put all the resources in my power to uncover who did this ugly desecration. Do you have any idea who might be behind it?"

"None."

"Any Klansman up here?"

"Probably some sympathizers. I don't know of an organized group."

"Trooper, would you get on the radio and request the Sheriff and the Chief come over here to the scene?"

"Right away, sir."

"Did they respond earlier?"

"I couldn't say."

"Those peckerwoods better be there when I get there!"

When they pulled up, no one was present except some of the church members walking around with lanterns looking for any portion of the symbols of their faith, which might have survived the blaze. The structure was totally gone.

"Wonder if they had any insurance, Fred?"

"Homer, what do you think?"

"Where will they meet?"

"Perhaps one of the other churches."

"Don't you have an auditorium over at the college?"

Almost insulted, Fred responded, "Certainly, Homer, we are not some hick college in Mississippi."

"There is a lot about this that looks like Mississippi to me."

"Where are the cops in this county? Boyce-trooper did you tell them to get over here? That I did not have all night to deal with this situation?"

"Yessir."

"Call em again and don't mince words."

Within minutes, they showed up in the Sheriff's car.

"Good evening Sheriff—Chief. Since no one is on the scene can I assume that you have solved this crime?"

"Evening, Governor. Not yet, sir."

"How do we know it was a crime, sir?" asked the Sheriff.

"Have you called the state fire marshal? Are you out rounding up suspects? Have you questioned witnesses before the trail gets cold?"

"Dang, Homer, it's just a nigger church. We'll be on it tomorrow."

"Sheriff, I am the Governor of Indiana! The Number One Law Enforcement Officer of this whole danged state. Unless you get on this tonight and don't stop until you've solved it, your ass is going to be in a sling. You will be the only sheriff in Indiana who has no authority. You hear me?"

"If you say so, Governor."

"If you don't say so you are going to be on the street looking for a job. Listen up, General Smythe will be here within the hour with a Military Police Unit from the Guard. He will maintain law and order. You remember the riots they had in Detroit and Washington. Well, we are not going to have any of those. Your officers and all of the sheriffs deputies will be assigned full time duty searching for who did this—Klansmen, Klan sympathesizers, race baiters, trouble-makers—anybody with dirty hands on this deal—anybody! Collier County is now under martial law and we will not have any problems. Do I make myself clear? Now get about it."

"Fred, do you have any empty dorm rooms or is there a little hotel I can hang out in for a few days?"

"Let's go see what's available, Governor."

The governor shouted to the sheriff as he was almost to his vehicle, "One of you stay here and take command! Get some officers here for a while or until General Smythe relieves them. Got that?" he said sternly. "Got that?"

"Yessir, Governor."

"That pissant can call me Homer at a fundraiser, but when I'm on the job I want respect."

"Aren't you being a little tough on the guy, Homer?"

"You heard the bastard, 'just a nigger church." He hasn't seen tough yet. I only want cops who treat all citizens with respect, to hell with the rest of them."

Chapter Forty-Three

The General Arrives
Thursday, April 18, 1935

General Smythe arrived with about forty Military Police personnel. He had his men dressed in regular trooper uniforms so they wouldn't alarm the citizens on the Hill. No helmets or riot gear, just two-piece khaki outfits carrying only a nightstick. Their headgear was a wide-brimmed field hat. They looked like Boy Scouts. The men were there to direct traffic, handle emergencies and help where they could. The local deputies and city police were assigned to work on the arson case full time.

A little after midnight on the morning of the eighteenth of April the Governor called all of them together in a large classroom at the college. He had written one word on the chalkboard—

NIGGER.

As they filed in, the room became as quiet as an empty church. Not a word was spoken until Homer Beasley stood to address the group.

"Have any of you in this room used this word in the last week? If so raise your hand."

He raised his hand. A few more did. The Chief did not raise his hand.

"I raised my hand because I used this word twice within the last two hours," the governor acknowledged soberly. Some of the men chuckled.

"I was repeating what I heard one of you in this room say about the building which is now the center of a serious crime. That word was used as an adjective to describe that church building where almost forty citizens of Collier County were injured, some seriously, and scores more escaped with their lives." He paused and scanned the room, looking into the eyes of every man. "But it cannot happen again in our State of Indiana on my watch," he continued dramatically raising the volume of his voice but slowing his words for effect. "We will apprehend the thugs who perpetrated this crime and they will be punished to the full extent of the law."

"One more thing, do not ever use that word again while you are on duty enforcing the law in Indiana. I know it is not against any law of the state. Nevertheless, it is against the rules—MY RULES—that clear? Do you understand?" And with that, he strode over to the board and erased the nasty word. "It's history here in Indiana. Got that?"

A calm Governor Beasley then said, "Would Sheriff Peale and Chief Mankiwitz come up along with General Smythe."

"To those of you who don't know these people, this is General Smythe, Sheriff Peale and Chief Mankiwitz."

Governor Beasley quietly explained his plan.

Smythe would be in charge of law enforcement for the entire county—with the sheriff and chief reporting directly to him. Their men would search every nook and cranny of the territory to uncover suspects, round them up and bring them for questioning in a temporary facility at the college. The State Fire Marshall would be down by dawn to supervise the investigation of the crime scene. Lastly, Governor Beasley announced that the county would remain under martial law until after Easter weekend. General Smythe was to set up blockades and request the drivers of all cars to stop and allow a voluntary search as well as voluntarily giving the destination and ID of each passenger. Those who were willing to do so were passed and any others were detained briefly for serious questioning. All other business would go on as usual.

A member of the guard detachment was a detective in Indianapolis. He briefed the search team with a profile of potential suspects:

- Known race baiters
- Known or suspected arsonists in the area
- Klan members and their family
- Young to middle aged whites recently in town from Evansville or other places where the Klan had been active in the last few years
- Known political enemies of county or city leaders involved in the annexation deal
- Persons known to display battle emblems of the old Confederacy
- Jobless men who fear that some of the colored might take employment from them

He dismissed the men and told the officers to report to him at ten a.m. every morning with a list of potential suspects--including full demographic information on each suspect. He asked the police chief to assign four local police officers to question every business in town including schools and churches about any threats or employees who did not show up for work today. They would report to him at the end of the day.

He also asked President Trotman to check the roll at the school to see who didn't show up for class.

Chapter Forty-Four

Bad Things Happen to Good People- Again
Thursday, April 18, 1935

"President Eakerly, please—"

"Dr. Eakerly, this is Fred Trotman in Fort Anthony."

"Well, I'm fine. I'm calling about Ezra Temple.—Well, ah, sadly we had a fire here last night and Ez was burned quite badly."

"No, not his house, at his church."

"No, I understand his hands are not burned."

"Can you find his mother and have her call my office here in Fort Anthony–Main 1096?"

"I'll know more when she calls. Thanks, yes, good-bye."

The State Fire Marshall nodded to his two assistants and began to inspect the scene. "From your description and the physical evidence, it clearly appears to be arson. Let us look around a bit." An empty fuel can was laying about thirty feet from the corner of the church building where the fire started. The cross once laden with fuel soaked rags was still standing although heavily charred. The bark was still on what had been a black locust sapling. It was green enough not to be flammable. Some of the rags, which had been wrapped around the cross, appeared to be hotel towels or towels from a linen service. The telltale odor of both coal oil and gasoline were still evident.

Fire Marshall Avery declared the fire to have been the work of an arsonist. His technicians would examine what was left of the exploded can to check any identifying marks. The towel fragments were to be checked with linen services, any hotel or overnight facility around, for the source. He asked Governor Beasley to keep him informed of any evidence uncovered away from the crime scene.

Esther called President Trotman's office back within thirty minutes. He told her the story, at least what he knew so far. She broke down with grief and ZD took the phone. "Should I bring her up there?"

"When? Okay. When can she talk to Ez? Okay, I'll have her at the house at 6:30 waiting on his call." He gave Trotman the number and thanked him for the call.

"Vern, this is Fred Trotman. It is not your fault, Vern! We all wanted to help them."

"Vern, what I called about is the Governor wants a place for Hannibal's church to meet for all their services this weekend—They have a Maundy Thursday foot washing, a Good Friday evening communion and an Easter service on Sunday."

"He asked me if we had an auditorium. They can use that if they wish. Think about it and call me back."

"Dr. Griffin, please, –Charley this is Fred Trotman—you folks were great last night,–still got a full house,–Governor Beasley was sure impressed this morning when we had breakfast. I know that's a problem—I'll talk to him about that. He will get the money somewhere. Charley, I promised Ez Temple's mother that he would call her at six-thirty tonight. Can you work that out? I will be there and will bring Homer with me. Fine, see you then."

Chapter Forty-Five

The Investigation
Maundy Thursday Afternoon, April 18, 1935

About three thirty Governor Homer Beasley walked into the office of President Fred Trotman.

"Fred, we've got a problem. The Fire Marshall tells me that the rags, which were burning on the cross, seem to be from your linen service here at the school."

"Homer, what the devil are you talking about? Do you suspect it was one of my staff or a student?"

"No one else in town uses it and they confirmed from the labels and quality that it is their stuff. He needs to talk to you. Do you have a minute?"

"Certainly."

Marshall Avery and his two assistants joined the two somber men in the President's office. Avery spoke in an equally somber tone.

"Dr. Trotman, do you know of anyone who would have bad feelings towards anyone who was at the church that night?"

"That's a frightening question, we have several hundred students and staff here, and I am sure that from time to time disagreements arise but not to that level. Do you think somebody here could have done this?"

"The linen service identified the rags used to burn the cross as towels from the stock they supply this campus. This campus is the only customer they have around here."

"Perhaps they got the towels from some other town."

"Possible, but not likely. This looks and feels like a local matter. We would like to question some others but only with your permission."

"We will certainly cooperate, but I would like to avoid a big uproar on my campus. How do you want to start?"

"Our investigators will begin immediately. Could you call a meeting of your staff?"

"Of course and please keep me informed as you proceed."

"Gladly."

The marshall and his deputies had been busy scouring the scene for clues. Having the towels, the fuel cans and having interviewed the able bodied and most observant persons, they found, they left to return to Indianapolis taking the evidence with them.

It was the Governor who spoke next. "Fred don't get your drawers in a wad. He has a job to do."

"Sure, Homer, but I have a job to do as well."

At six p.m. Early came down to the home of Esther Temple to remind her it was time to be up at the President's house for a phone call from Ez. It was decided that she should not take the call by herself at her house. She asked Early to stay with Easy while she walked up the hill. The days were getting much longer and there was some daylight left. Esther had noted an unfamiliar car earlier that day but thought nothing of it. On the short walk up the hill she saw it again slowly passing her headed down the hill. She noticed the South Carolina plates but nothing else as she walked along at a deliberate pace. She thought to herself "I should have driven up here."

The three were sitting in the parlor awaiting the call when the phone rang. Dr. Eakerly took the call.

"Hello?" It was Early.

"Yes. I'll call security."

"Two men just broke into your house and kidnapped Easy!"

Esther flew out the door and ran down the hill screaming, "Easy, Easy, my baby, oh Easy, what have I done? Oh, my child!" Esther prayed as she stumbled down the hill." "Oh God, save my child, oh, Jesus forgive me, oh, Jesus, what can I do? Oh Lord, I need Your help!"

ZD called campus security, who in turn called the police, who called the FBI about the kidnapping, now a federal crime. Within minutes, the FBI called to confirm that the State Police had set up roadblocks. Early added, "There were two of them and did not say a word but snatched Easy from his seat at the piano and ran to the car."

The phone rang in the entry hall of the home of ZD and Becca Eakerly but no one answered.

Chapter Forty-Six

Spreading the Word
Good Friday, April 19, 1935

ZD immediately put in a call to the home of Fred Trotman in Fort Anthony. The line was busy. He hung up and immediately rang the operator.

"Mary, this is an emergency call."

He gave her the number and she asked Long Distance to break in to the call.

Ellie answered sounding a little frightened "Hello, yes Dr. Eakerly." She almost fainted when he told her the grim news.

"Fred is at the hospital with Ezra attempting to call you. No, I do not have that number but if you will give me your number, I will find him and call you back."

Ellie drove by to pick up Rose and check on Randy. She did not know if she had the strength to do the job ahead alone.

She hurriedly went in the kitchen door where Randy, covered with gauze, was having some soup.

"Hi Randy, is Rose here?"

Rose hearing the voices came into the breakfast room. "You are out of breath, Ellie."

Ellie told her why and asked if she would join her on the sad mission.

Randy was in tears as the two ladies drove off to the hospital.

Within minutes after the FBI called for roadblocks all over eastern Kentucky and West Virginia, the Troopers were stopping every car searching for Easy and his captors. They recognized that a change of cars could have been made or that the abductors could have holed up somewhere until the heat was off.

At four a.m. on April 19, Good Friday, on a flat straightaway of Highway 31 E near the Kentucky/Tennessee line, a new Ford sedan pulled from a back road onto the highway and poured on the gas to the little 85 horsepower V-8 engine. The anxious driver was determined to make the Tennessee border before being stopped by a Kentucky Trooper. About a hundred yards short of his goal the bright lights of four Highway Patrol cars shined toward him. They signaled him to stop. He blew through the lights and across the state line and on toward Lafayette, then towards Gallatin, Tennessee, with his precious cargo. He was almost into Lafayette when more lights came on, and he saw a barricade set up in his path. The child in the seat beside him was screaming bloody murder. At eighty miles an hour, he could crash the barricade and perhaps escape one more trap. On the other hand, he could kill them all in a wreck and ruin the car. He slowed down and told his accomplices to jump and run and leave him with the boy. He stopped about a hundred feet short of the troopers. The two men jumped out disappearing into the darkness. The driver started moving slowly and came to a stop at the barricade. With guns drawn, the troopers approached him.

"Step out of the car please." He did and was frisked.

"Where you going this time of the night in such a hurry?"

"To Gallatin, Tennessee, to take this boy to see his grandma."

Another trooper stepped from behind the car and said, "He's got South Carolina plates."

"Who's his Grandma?"

"Mrs. Love."

"Delilah Love's mother."

"Yessir."

"We'll take care of that. You have a date with the FBI."

Chapter Forty-Seven

On The Mend
Friday, April 19, 1935

Ez spent a restless night, even with the help of a mild sedative. Vern and other ministers, students and friends sat with him every night and all day. It was a joint decision to avoid sharing the news about Easy until he was stronger. There was nothing to be gained and a lot to be lost. He needed his strength to recover.

The New Awakenings Baptist Church met for their Wednesday evening foot washing service under a small tent provided by the Dobbs Funeral Home with the elders and some of the infirm sisters sitting on folding chairs from the same source. The evening was clear and cool. Several ministers of other churches in town shared the pastoral duties and a large crowd of Christians was present, some to observe, some to wash the feet of their neighbors.

Word of the apprehension of the abductor of Easy Temple first reached Fort Anthony in a message to Governor Homer Beasley. A Quaker, he sought a private place to meditate and offer a prayer to Almighty God for the grace showered on his people. He walked into Fred Trotman's office to break the news.

"They got him."

"The child?'

"Yes and his Uncle Samson confessed to the abduction and, astonishingly, some involvement in the church burning."

"What was the motive? I didn't even know that Ez had a brother-in-law."

"It seems that the child's other grandmother was very upset with her son-in-law. She believes Ezra is responsible for the death of her daughter and her baby. She hates him for his failure to bring the boy with him for the funeral of the boy's mother. Hates him for leaving before the burial and, according to the mother, he has hidden the boy away beyond her reach."

"Sounds to me like she had reason to be upset."

"But not to conspire in burning down a church and the kidnapping of a child."

"Why did she want to burn down the church?"

"We don't know yet."

"Where is the boy?"

"In the custody of Tennessee Welfare Department."

"What will they do with him?"

"I would imagine they will examine the best alternatives for the boy. I think that will be in the custody of the father if he is well enough to care for him."

"He has a schedule that would kill a mule."

"What do you mean?"

Fred went on to describe the things they had worked out with the Indiana University School of Music, the load he had on campus here and his work at the church.

"What kind of house does he have?"

"It's pretty rough. Over on Hardscuffle and without water and indoor plumbing."

"We need to talk about that. Do you have any faculty housing here on campus?"

"Some, but it's full."

"What about a small house here in town?"

"In a white neighborhood?"

"Do you have any colored living in town?"

"No, only on Hardscuffle Road in the county."

"See if you can rent suitable quarters adjacent to the campus until a faculty house becomes available."

"We'll try our best."

The questioning by the FBI agents continued for most of the morning. Samson was exhausted and soon gave up. He poured out his many reasons to the agents.

He felt like Ez had mistreated his sister and caused her death. Samson hated Ez.

He felt like Ez had mistreated his mother. She hated Ez. Samson said he did not know the names of his two accomplices. He called them Luke and John. He hired them off the street in Indianapolis. They were two white guys who were out of work and needed money. He gave them twenty dollars on the spot and promised them ten bucks a day for the job. He says they were armed and forced him to drop them out at the Tennessee Highway Patrol roadblock. He stayed at the Colored YMCA in Indianapolis where he got the towels. They brought the cans and the coal oil and gasoline.

He says he only wanted to burn a cross to frighten folks who were associated with Ez. Luke and John set the church on fire. They were drunk and acted crazy about half the time. He says he did not kidnap Easy. He was taking him back to his grandmother where he belonged. Luke or John acquired the South Carolina tags in Indianapolis. His mother did not know he was doing this. He wanted her to love him as much as she loved his sister Delilah, so he did this to please her and win her affection.

After Samson completed the nonstop confession, the agents let him rest in a cell and went to the home of his mother.

"Mrs. Love, I am FBI Special Agent Looney from Nashville, Tennessee. This is Special Agent Douglas. Could we come in?"

"What for?"

"We need to ask you a few questions."

"About what?"

"About the whereabouts of your son."

"He's at work in Nashville--at the railroad. "

"What does he do for the railroad?"

"Works."

"What kind of work, Mrs. Love?"

"I don't know. Is he in trouble?"

"We think so. Did he mention any travel plans to you?"

"He's a grown man with a good job, a good car, and good place to live in Nashville. He comes to see me about every two weeks or so. We go to church and then we have lunch together."

"When did you see him last?"

"He's coming up here for Easter, so it must have been almost two weeks ago."

"Where does he live in Nashville, ma'am?"

"South, I think?"

"South what, Ma'am?"

"South Nashville. Didn't you say you were from Nashville? You know where working colored folks live. He lives on Division Street I think. If you want to know anything else you better ask him." She slammed the door.

"What do you think, Looney?"

"I think she may be telling the truth."

Chapter Forty-Eight

A Joint Effort
Good Friday Afternoon, April 19, 1935

General Smythe called his brigade commander, the sheriff and the police chief into his temporary office.

"Gentlemen, I want to thank you on behalf of Governor Beasley and the people of Indiana for the exemplary manner with which you and your troops have conducted themselves during this emergency. In unsettled times like these we never know when an everyday occurrence will blow up in our faces. I don't mean to say this was an everyday thing but because of your good work, it came out fine. The leader of the gang who perpetrated this heinous crime has been apprehended, and we will eventually apprehend the other two. Thank you all. Please pass my commendation along to your men. Please dismiss your men so they can return to their families and their regular duties."

Homer Beasley went by the hospital to visit the victims who remained. He stopped in Ez Temple's room and sat beside the bed. He held the young man's hand and said a brief prayer.

"Professor, this has been a tough couple of days for many of us. Your full return to health is of utmost concern to me. I will arrange for your transfer to the burn unit at the State Medical School Hospital. I want them to analyze your situation so I can be certain you are getting the treatment you need. Dr. Trotman is arranging for you to move into faculty housing when you are well enough to leave. I am going to send a driver to bring your mother and son up to visit you wherever you may be. I think that it might be good for her to come up here with your son and live in the new residence with you. Know that you have made many friends in this state and I am one of them. I am going back to Indianapolis this afternoon, but I will keep a close eye on your progress. Good Luck."

Ez looked him in the eye and said, "Thanks, Governor Beasley I am proud to be a citizen of your state. You are a good man."

Next, the Governor went to the office of the administrator of the hospital.

"Doctor, I know you have expended a considerable amount of your resources on this latest tragedy. I will see that you are reimbursed for all your costs and that of the physicians and other professionals who were so helpful that night. I want Ez Temple transferred to Indiana University Medical just to be sure he is getting all that modern medicine can provide. He has great promise and I want to see him blossom. Will that be okay with you?"

"Of course, Governor. You might want to check with IU Medical to see if they might want to send a team over here. It could be safer for the patient."

"Good thinking, contact them and tell them I said to do what the two of you agree is best for the patient."

Homer Beasley's last stop was to see Hannibal Hayes when he assured the minister that the college facilities were available to the congregation to use for as long as they needed. "Just call President Trotman. I have spoken to him and he is okay with the plan. If any of your members need additional medical attention, call the Hospital Administration office and talk to Dr. Charles Griffin. He is the Medical Director there."

He gave the minister a bear hug and Hannibal Hayes said simply

"Keep us in your prayers."

Beasley moved toward the Packard and said, "Okay, Big Bud, let's roll!" And roll they did!

Chapter Forty-Nine

The Department of Welfare Steps In
Saturday, April 20, 1935

Miss Elizabeth Johnson was a social worker for the Tennessee Department of Welfare. She had taken Easy to Nashville. He spent the days and nights with Mattie and Will, a colored family who lived on the corner of Edgehill Avenue and Villa Place across from The White Way Laundry. They were beloved servants in her parents' home just around the corner on 16th Ave South. Miss Johnson felt that he would be more comfortable there. Will and Mattie were tender with the child and Miss Johnson's parents were glad to have him about for a few days.

It was Saturday afternoon. Miss Johnson's nieces and nephews had come over to their Grandmother Johnson's house for dinner. The grandchildren looked forward to the chance to play with the young colored boy Aunt Elizabeth had brought home.

He quickly discovered the baby grand piano in the front room of the house and asked "Miss Maude" if he could play on it. She loved music and sat down with him to show him how. She was delighted at his skill, so when the company arrived she was full of herself at having discovered this prodigy. The kids wanted to go play on the sidewalk but had to hear him play the piano. They said he was good.

Will announced that dinner was served. Grandfather Johnson's grandchildren were around him. He lovingly helped each deal with the knives and forks around their plate. He was a very sad man, broken from the economic ravages of the Great Depression. After a supper of fried chicken, cornbread and vegetables (canned from last years crop) which Mattie had lovingly prepared on the wood burning cook stove, the children were allowed to go out to play on the sidewalk.

Soon the old gentleman appeared, rose from his solitaire game in the library, to walk with the children to the corner drugstore to get an ice cream cone. The boys agreed to take the girls along. The children were especially good, since they were looking for gifts from the Easter Bunny. The children went home and to bed early and so did Easy. They were all hastened along so they could get to bed early and ready for the Sunrise Service in the big park the next morning. They were all treated the same. Easy went to the Easter Service surrounded by dozens of white families who went to great lengths to make him feel loved.

CHAPTER FIFTY

Easter Morning
Sunday, April 21, 1935

The sun on Easter Morning rose to find scores of worshippers at the little park at the end of Hardscuffle Road near Fort Anthony, Indiana. The service began when the group of Christians gathered at the foot of the hill and walked to the ridge overlooking the town to the west and the rising sun to the east. It was difficult afoot and only the most hardhearted among them failed to notice their near squalid surroundings. As they walked up the hill, singing and rejoicing, colored neighbors were encouraged to join them, and when they arrived at the top, there was a good crowd.

Vern Shipley read the Easter Story; the morning prayer offered by Jim Bartley and the homily was given by Bishop Hannibal Hayes. The a capella choir sang "Fairest Lord Jesus" led by Lady Frances Hayes. They all joined in singing "Up from the Grave He Arose."

When the service was completed, they walked down the hill continuing to sing of the "Risen Christ" and how He defeated death and sin.

Later the congregation of the New Awakenings Baptist Church assembled at the auditorium on the campus of the College. They were welcomed by the President and a letter of greeting and an expression of sorrow from the Governor Homer Beasley. There was no organ but there was a small grand piano and it had been tuned in anticipation of this event. The service was a joyful one and the cause for celebration overshadowed any sadness caused by events of the previous week.

The service went on into the afternoon.

The Congregation of the First Methodist Church conducted their Easter service with the usual overflow crowd. They sang the usual songs, took up the usual offering, prayed the usual prayers and sat back for the usual sermon.

The text was the story of the Good Samaritan. Not his usual Easter Text. The sermon was short and to the point:

"In the parable of the Good Samaritan Jesus answers the question posed by the lawyer who was asking help in defining the limits of his neighborhood. In the context of the affairs of the day, Jesus said that there is no limit to the size of our neighborhood."

"Here in Fort Anthony," continued The Reverend Shipley, "we are learning this lesson. What affects our neighbors on Hardscuffle Road and what some call Nigger Hill affects us and we must bind up the wounds of our neighbors wherever we find them no matter their race, color or creed."

"On this Easter Sunday," spoke the preacher earnestly, "we need to learn one greater lesson from His suffering on the Cross at Calvary. He sacrificed for us today. He gave his life for us. He expanded our understanding of neighborliness. By His supreme act of out-reaching love, He demonstrated His eternal love for us. Today our lesson is that we must love our neighbors across time as well. To love them, to cherish them, and to share God's gifts with them forever."

"I hold this to be a self-evident truth: Our descendants will be here on this earth through all the millennium to follow, long after we are gone. The only way we can show compassion to them is to leave them a decent place to live and decent folks with whom to live. Not only will they be our collective descendants but also our collective neighbors across time."

* "Throughout our adventure, our primary purpose has been to be Disciples of Jesus Christ, to keep the peace, to foster progress in human achievement, and to enhance liberty, dignity and integrity among peoples and among nations. To strive for less would be unworthy of a free and religious people.

We—you and I, must avoid the impulse to live only for today, plundering, for our own ease and convenience, the precious resources of tomorrow.

We cannot mortgage the material assets of our grandchildren without risking the loss also of their spiritual heritage. We want our Christian heritage and culture to survive for all generations to come, not to become the phantom of tomorrow.

Down the long lane of the history yet to be written, we know that this land of ours, ever growing smaller, must avoid becoming a community of dreadful fear and hate, and be instead, a proud confederation of mutual trust and respect.

We need to be strong in our faith that all persons of good will, under God, will reach the goal of justice for all our neighbors. May we be unswerving in devotion to this principle, confident but humble, diligent in pursuit of these great goals."

"Will you pray with me:

We pray that peoples of all faiths, all races, all nations, may have their great human needs satisfied; that those now denied opportunity shall come to enjoy it to the fullest; that all who yearn for freedom may experience its spiritual blessings, that those who have freedom will understand, also, its heavy responsibility; that all who are insensitive to the needs of others, will learn charity, and that the scourges of poverty, disease and ignorance will be made to disappear from the earth; and that in the goodness of time, all people will come to live together in a peace guaranteed by the binding force of mutual respect and love. In the name of the Prince of Peace and the Arbiter of Justice, we offer this prayer. Amen."

*Used by permission of the Eisenhower Library. From the Farewell Address of President Eisenhower in January 1961. Written by Dr. Malcolm Moos who later became President of the University of Minnesota.

Chapter Fifty-One

The Dreaded Bureaucracy
Monday, April 22, 1935

On Monday, Elizabeth Johnson received a call from Dr. Z.D. Eakerly, President of Eastern Kentucky Agricultural School.

"Miss Johnson, I understand the State of Tennessee has taken custody of a youngster who was abducted from the home of his grandmother here on our campus. What is the procedure we need to follow to facilitate his return to his home?"

"I see."

"When can you do that?"

"Where is he now?"

"Can we come to see him?"

"Why not?"

"Miss Johnson this is very hard on his grandmother."

"His father has been badly burned and is in a hospital in Fort Anthony, Indiana, and she wishes to visit her son and take his child when she goes."

"She would like to go up this weekend."

"Miss Johnson, the child has lost his mother recently, been dislocated, has lost his grandfather and been kidnapped by his uncle. His father has been badly injured in arson of the church they attend and we all need to do what we can to bring this family together again. I trust we can all work together to make this happen as expeditiously as possible. The Governor of Indiana is doing all in his power; the President of Western Indiana State Teachers College is doing all he can do. The Minister at the Fort Anthony First Methodist Church is doing his part, and I would surely appreciate it if you would find a way to be cooperative in this matter."

"Yes, I will. Thank you. Goodbye."

Becca and Esther were standing close by. "What did she say?" they asked in unison.

"She said she would call me back."

"But you did not give her your number!"

"Well, then I'll call her back" was his very frustrated response.

Miss Johnson had to prepare a detailed report for whoever would make the final decisions or in case of some involvement of a court to make the decisions, a written record would be required. No doubt, the father had rightful possession of the child and she would need to relinquish Easy back to him soon. What about the conflicting interests of the grandmothers? Where was his Grandmother Temple when he was abducted? Did his Grandmother Love know of the plans of the kidnapping? Was the father well enough to care for the child without some help? Would the grandmother move from her home in Kentucky to Indiana to care for the child? What does the child think?

On Monday, she talked to the FBI Agent Looney who said he was not sure about the involvement of Grandmother Love. There was certainly a lot of hatred for the father by the folks in Gallatin. The Federal Grand Jury would solve many of those questions. That would take a while. He suggested that the child go back to his father as soon as possible.

She talked to the father's employer, Dr. Fred Trotman. He assured her that Ezra Temple was a conscientious man who he would trust absolutely. He had received orders from the Governor to find faculty housing for Ezra, suitable to raise the child. Although he had not met

Mrs. Temple, he understood from Dr. Eakerly that she was a rock and would continue to be an exemplary mother figure for the child.

Miss Johnson also talked to Dr. Eakerly who explained that Mrs. Temple had walked to his house to take a phone call from her son in the hospital and his man Early Owens was at the house when the boy was abducted. She asked if Mrs. Temple could pull up stakes and move to Indiana to live with her son and take care of Easy there. He told her that although she was a schoolteacher in the public schools that he would work with her superintendent to facilitate a quick move if Miss Johnson thought it best.

She left the State Office Building on Cedar Street and drove out to her home on Sixteenth Avenue South. She wanted to interview Easy before she completed her report. She found him at the piano and sat with him for a minute listening to his latest composition.

"Easy, I have talked to your Dr. Eakerly—"

"You mean Dr. Z.D.?"

That was strange she thought, "Yes Dr. Z.D. Eakerly, the President of the school where you live."

"How's my Grandmama?"

"She's fine."

"Tell me about your life with your Grandmama."

He described in detail their daily rituals, up early, good breakfast, off to school, home, snack, music lessons, spelling and reading. Work in the garden, fishing with Early, supper with Evelyn and Early up at the presidents house, "I played the piano for them, too," he said proudly.

She went to the phone in the upstairs hall and put in a call to Dr. Eakerly to ask for Esther's phone number if she had one. She did and called Esther Temple.

"Mrs. Temple, this is Elizabeth Johnson, a social worker with the Department of Welfare in Nashville, Tennessee. As you know, we have your grandchild in state custody after a very harrowing and frightful experience."

"Yes, he is fine, excellent in every respect. I commend you for your good work with him since his mother's death."

"Yes, he seems to be an exceptional child."

"Yes ma'am, we will decide quickly as to the disposition of this case." She knew she had limited power but was anxious to check out every angle.

"Yes, ma'am, yes ma'am. The child needs to be with his father but he needs a mother figure, a role which I understand you have been fulfilling very well."

"Yes, ma'am. Mrs. Temple would you consider moving to Fort Anthony, Indiana, to live with your son and take care of Easy."

"I understand from President Trotman that he will have faculty housing for your family."

"Yes, ma'am. It will be furnished and ready for occupancy fairly soon."

"The sooner the better. Yes, ma'am. Will you get back to me on this?"

"Call me at my office this afternoon. Elizabeth Johnson in Nashville at State 5551. Thank you, goodbye."

Chapter Fifty-Two

A Crucial Visit
Tuesday Morning, April 23, 1935

As she parked the car on the road in front of the little house where Delilah Love Temple had grown up, Miss Johnson felt some trepidation. She had brought Easy Temple with her, unannounced, to see his maternal grandmother. She braced herself, took Easy by the hand and knocked on the door.

"Mrs. Love?"

"Yes, I'm Etta Mae Love."

"Mrs. Love, I am Elizabeth Johnson with the Tennessee

Department of Welfare. This is Ezra Nehemiah Temple Jr. who I believe is your grandson."

With that, Etta Mae swooned and fell to the floor.

"Looks like we surprised her," said Easy.

"Easy, you sit over there in the swing and I will go in and see about Mrs. Love."

Miss Johnson went in the house and to the kitchen to get a cold damp cloth. A young colored man was sitting frozen in a kitchen chair at the table. He did not say a word. He was like an ebony statue in a ladder back chair. She picked up a cloth and dampened it in a water pitcher and went back to the front door to examine Grandma Love. By this time, the old lady was beginning to recover. The cool cloth helped her regain her wits.

"Mrs. Love, it is okay. I am only here for a brief visit. We wanted you to see your grandson before we take him back to his father."

Mrs. Love sat up. A frail little woman who obviously feared authority, "You gonna take him away, too? They taken Samson. Delilah's dead. Her baby died, too. The Germans killed my Frank, and you goin' to take my little baby away and I'll never see him again."

"Mrs. Love, we need to get you to a doctor. When have you eaten anything?"

"I ain't got nothing to eat. Samson got all my money and said he would pay off this boy's daddy to get him to let him come home to me. I ain't got no money, no food, nobody. I'm dying of a broken heart. I don't need no food. You go on. Take him back to his daddy and his daddy's mama. They got plenty. They got each other and I ain't got nobody, no thing, just a broken heart. You go on let me die by myself."

"Mrs. Love, who is that I saw in the kitchen just now?"

"He ain't nobody. I don't know him. He just came by to talk. You leave him alone. He ain't nobody!"

"Easy, come with me. Mrs. Love please come with me. I think I should go to the police."

"You go on honey, I'm okay."

Elizabeth came back with the chief of police.

"Mrs. Love this is Charley Goins, I'm coming in."

"What you want, Charley? I didn't call you."

"Mrs. Love is Little Jimmy bothering you again?"

"It ain't none of yoah business. Now you go on away Charley. I'll be alright."

"Mrs. Love we can help you if you let us."

"You go on now Charley. If I need you I'll call you."

"Yes Mrs. Love. Have a good day."

"Ma'am, Mrs. Love is in bad shape but I can't do nothing about it. We try but she gives her food away to Little Jimmy Eads and she is starving. But he keeps her company and she is lonesome. I think she is losing it, myself."

Elizabeth put Easy back in the car and headed to Richmond, Kentucky.

"I'll come back and try to help her later."

Chapter Fifty-Three

Plans for the Widow and Orphan
Later in the afternoon
April 23, 1935

"Dr. Eakerly, I am Elizabeth Johnson. We spoke on the phone the other day."

"Come in; come in. Where is Easy?"

"He is in the car waiting for me. What is the situation with Mrs. Temple and her transfer to Fort Anthony?"

"We've made arrangements for her move to Fort Anthony. She will teach at the college demonstration school on the campus. Ez will be home next week and she will nurse him at home. They will have a nice room for Easy and he can go to the kindergarten at the school. She will teach music at the school and continue to work with Easy in his lessons"

"You've tied up a lot of loose ends since we talked."

"This is important, Miss Johnson."

"I understand, Dr. Eakerly."

"Can I see Mrs. Temple?"

"Can I see Easy?"

"Sure, Easy would you come here please?"

The child ran to the door and hugged Dr. Eakerly around the knees. "I'm really glad to be home!"

"We're really glad to have you home, Easy." He picked up the little boy and hugged him ferociously.

"Can I see Grandmama, please?"

"You sure can. I'll call her right now."

Elizabeth said, "I would like to visit the home here."

"Surely, I'll get the car."

"I'll take mine."

"Why not walk down?"

"Fine."

Elizabeth lit up a Philip Morris and headed out. The trip back to Lexington went through Boonesboro and Athens. She was fascinated with the countryside, the horse farms and the quaint little towns. She stayed the night in Lexington. The next morning she decided to go out to Lealand Farms and take in a race. The Spring Meet had begun. She thought "Ah me, a mint julep and a day at the track to heal the hurting heart." The Department of Welfare could wait for their star social worker for a day or two.

After a day for things to settle down and some preparation Esther and Easy were ready to go to Fort Anthony. Z.D. and Rebecca had a farewell dinner for them. He invited Esther and Job's old friends, and Easy played the piano for all to enjoy. The next day they set out in the Peerless automobile with which Z.D. had endowed them. The car was in perfect condition with its Straight Line, eight cylinder Continental engine, it was the most dependable car on the road. It was still running great after several years of use. All their possessions were carefully packed in the back seat and in the canvas covered nickel chrome trimmed trunk on the rear fold down rack. The tires had been checked, the oil level was fine, the gas tank filled. Z.D. had given Easy a nice cash gift and paid Esther a small bonus for things she had done around the campus since Job had passed away.

Fort Anthony, Indiana or bust!

Chapter Fifty-Four

Getting Down to Business
Friday, April 26, 1935

Rose Roberts and Ellie Trotman met for lunch before visiting the hospital.

"How is Randy?" Ellie asked.

"He is getting better every day. He is still not comfortable with a suit and tie."

"He is looking after his business by telephone and you know as well as I do that Roberta Cummins practically runs the bank. He has asked Louise Edwards to look after the city for him."

"I bet she loves that."

"Absolutely. She thinks she runs the place anyway. What are we going to do about the Mayday Musical that Ez has planned?"

"What do you mean 'we' Rose?"

"Well, we should talk to him about it when we visit this afternoon."

"How is he? Have you seen him lately?'

"I see him every day. However, we have not discussed any final plans. I tell him we will cross that bridge when we come to it. We are just about there."

"Does he know that his mother and son are on their way soon?"

"Yes, and he is delighted. Has Fred found him a house near the campus?"

"He's close. I believe one of the families who is currently occupying on-campus housing is leaving for greener pastures soon."

"That would be good. Is it big enough?"

"Fred thinks so."

They found Ez in better spirits. Rose had cut some daffodils and arranged them in a pitcher found in his room. He asked when he should expect his mother and Easy. He had talked to them by phone twice since Easy returned home but was not sure of their arrival time.

"We are not sure either. I would like to take Mary Ella over there and straighten up your house. I bet you went off and left it a mess."

"Afraid so. Somebody from the church could go by and do that."

"Well, I guess they could but nobody asked them and I am certain they are busy with other things. Where do you keep a key?"

"I never lock it. Folks over there won't bother anything and I don't have much worth locking up anyway."

Ellie jumped in, "what about the musical?"

"I suppose you should cancel it or put it off for a while."

"I'll talk to Fred and see what he thinks."

"I hope to be out of the hospital soon. The doctors have worked miracles. They are burn specialists and have some magic medicine they use. I am healing quickly."

"Randy said to ask you if you would like to have a radio or some records to listen to music. He has a new Benny Goodman record with Tim Wilson playing the piano."

"Tim Wilson, from Tuskegee?"

"I don't know. Do you know him?"

"I knew a Tim Wilson when we were kids. He played the piano when I was learning the clarinet. We jammed together as kids."

"I'll have Elder Ed Ricketts bring a radio and a phonograph over. I'll pick out some other music you might enjoy, too."

Chapter Fifty-Five

Later that day
Friday, April 26, 1935

"Randy, I'm going to send your radio and phonograph player over to Ez for a day or two. I think it will make him feel better. Do you mind if I send your new Benny Goodman record with Mr. Ricketts when he takes them?"

"Why don't you send him my right arm or the key to our bank box? I'm kidding. Sure, I think I'll ride with Ed when he goes."

"His mother is due this afternoon late, and I am taking Mary Ella over to straighten up his place. God only know what it looks like."

"Do you know where it is?"

"Mr. Ricketts can tell me."

"Why don't I go with you and Mary Ella and I will take the radio and stuff over tonight."

"Do you feel like it?"

"If you mean, do I feel like cleaning up anything the answer is no, but Ed can help and I can supervise."

"Why don't you just send Ed? I don't need another boss hanging around."

"I would really like to go."

"Well, come on."

After an early start, Esther and Easy turned on the radio in the car and listened to 50,000-watt clear channel WLAC in Nashville selling Pomade and baby chicks. They sang with the gospel groups. They tuned in to "Don McNeill's Breakfast Club" and listened to "Ma Perkins," "Shining Light" and the other morning soap operas as they could pick them up along the way. They made Louisville before noon, crossed the Ohio River into Jeffersonville, Indiana, and began to wind northwest toward the Wabash River and Fort Anthony. They stopped for a picnic lunch as they left Jeffersonville when they purchased some gasoline and checked the oil. Easy kicked the tires as he had seen Early do before they left and pronounced them to be in "A-1 shape." He had come to love Early and Vashti as much as he loved Dr. Z.D. and Miss Rebecca. He would miss them and hoped they would come visit soon.

They each purchased a cold drink, she got an RC and he selected a Dr. Pepper. "Is it 10, 2 or 4 Grandmama?" he asked.

"Right in between but you can have a Dr. Pepper anyway." She was amused by his wit.

She selected a Moon Pie and he asked for a Baby Ruth. Along with the ham sandwiches that Becca Eakerly prepared, they feasted.

"Law me, Miss Rose, this place is a mess. Ed you come on in here and start putting up this man's clothes."

"Ain't it just like a man to go off and leave his things strewn about the house like some hog at a slop-trough? Men are just no account!"

"Now, Mary Ella, he has not had the benefit of a good woman to look after him for a long time. You need to start looking for a good one for him soon."

"Law, Miss Rose, that girl ain't been dead for a more than six months."

"Well, you keep your eye out, Mary Ella."

Ed Ricketts heard the conversation and chuckled. "Why buy a cow when the milk is so cheap? They will be looking for him in the daytime with a flashlight. Every gal in Indiana would break her arm trying to catch him. He'll be knocking 'em off with a baseball bat."

After three hours, the little shack looked presentable. Rose had put some fresh spring flowers around; Ed swept the front porch, Randy stayed out of the way by driving himself to the store. Rose had prepared a list for milk, eggs, other groceries, a chunk of ice for the icebox, and some kindling for the cook stove. She also instructed him to go by the hardware store to get some new utensils, pots and pans, a new dipper and bucket for drinking water. He bought a Crosley radio and a little windup phonograph. After a quick stop at the music store, he headed back to Hardscuffle Road and the cleanup crew.

Rose gave him a big hug and said, "You are the sweetest man I have ever known!"

Chapter Fifty-Six

That Evening
Friday April 26, 1935

It was a long dull drive across Highway 50 to 231 and north to Fort Anthony. Esther had never seen so many square miles of dirt fields on both sides of the road. Winter wheat, rye, some fresh plowed and some already planted with corn, would they have too much rain or not enough? It was in the hands of Mother Nature now she thought. Job's garden would have been doing good now and the corn and beans, the peppers, the okra, the tomatoes, the squash and eggplant would be showing signs of a fine harvest in a few weeks. She missed Job, and she would miss Early, Vashti, ZD and Becca. They were the best. They were truly people of God. They could give love in abundance and accept it with grace.

She had mixed feelings about the life she and Easy would have in this unknown place. The college president had seemed to be very nice and helpful. She even heard from the Mayor's wife with her gracious phone call. Would these people be real or just an imitation of real? She would soon see.

The Burma Shave signs were becoming repetitive. No more tobacco barns, no more bourbon storage barns. Just plowed fields.

"How much further, Grandmama?"

"Not far, Easy." The last sign said 13 miles it seemed like 133.

"There it is, Grandmama. See the red light up in the sky. That's my friend. I think it is a monkey with red eyes. I see it every night when I go to sleep. See his eyes, now he blinks, now see them? Is it bedtime Grandmama? We're home Grandmama, I just know we're home. I want to see daddy."

He is tired, she thought. Talking baby talk is not like him. "We will go to the hospital to see Daddy first."

As they rolled into the Gulf Station on the edge of town, she relaxed for the first time in almost 12 hours. She asked for some gas, the restrooms and directions.

The long necked kid in coveralls answered, "We don't have any colored rest rooms."

"Can you tell me where the hospital is, please?"

He gave her curt directions. "Don't you want to know where Nigger Hill is now?" he asked with a snaggletooth grin.

"Just the hospital will be fine. Thank you."

She scratched off, leaving the pump attendant with the nozzle in his hand and a little gravel in his face. Things were not off to a great start in Fort Anthony, Indiana.

She drove to the hospital and asked for the number of Ezra's room. As she and Easy were leaving the information counter, the duty clerk said crisply, "The child cannot go to the room. They carry germs you know."

"Ma'am, we have driven for almost 13 hours to get here for him to see his daddy. Can we put a mask on him or something?"

"Is this Professor Temple's son?"

"Yes, ma'am."

"Are you his mother?"

"I am the mother of Ezra Temple, yes."

"I'm so sorry," gushed the clerk. "They have been awaiting you for several hours. Let me take you back immediately."

"That's better," thought Esther.

When they turned the corner to Ezra's room where a voice said, "Here they are! Here they are!"

Waiting on them was Rose and Randy, Fred and Ellie, Ladye Frances Hayes and Bishop Hayes. And Ez.

Chapter Fifty-Seven

The Healing Continues
May 1, 1935

The musical was postponed to correspond with the graduation celebration on Friday, the 17th of May. This gave Ez, his students and others extra time to prepare. It also assured a good crowd for their premiere production.

Ez remained in some discomfort but most of his burns were healing nicely. He was in excellent health, so he healed more quickly than most. His hands were not burned, so he returned to the keyboard with very little discomfort.

The presence of Little Ezra, or Easy as he wished to be called, and Ezra's mother made life happier by any measure. Esther had cleaned the house once more and made a home of it again. She continued to tutor Easy, confident that he would be ready for the first grade at the Demonstration School.

Ellie and Fred Trotman hosted a dinner party honoring Esther Temple, who turned out to be a sparkling dinner guest and a woman of considerable charm. The guest list included the Roberts, the Shipley's, Jim and Nelda Bartley, Bishop Hayes, and Louise and Reggie Edwards.

The topics of conversation included the upcoming graduation events, the ongoing improvements in the Pleasant Hill neighborhood, the investigation into the arson and of course Easy Temple. Esther had some bragging rights about her student and grandson and she exercised them. All three ministers invited her to come to church and bring Easy to Sunday school soon.

Mayor Roberts was back to full time duty now and scheduled a meeting with Judge Leach on the Pleasant Hill Project. The state highway department had dispatched a grader blade over to prepare the road for paving. The city had erected signs noting the new city limits, the typical project sign noting that this is a joint project of the state of Indiana, the Federal Government, the County of Collier, the city of Fort Anthony and a sign designating the new addition to the city as the Pleasant Hill neighborhood. A modest plan for the Pleasant Hill Park was in the works.

"Well, what do you think, now that you have a colored neighborhood in your town?"

"I think it's kind of nice, Judge. Are you happy I have it and you don't?"

"Don't matter either way," he lied. "What's your next move?"

"We need to approve the park plan, and get the CCC or CWA folks in here to build the rockwork and a picnic shelter. Many unmarked graves up there need a lot of work and research. We are going to mark the ones we are sure about. The plan calls for a double shot gravel road and the ditches to be cleared and some culverts, not much more."

"You gonna plant any trees?"

"Some but that may have to wait."

"Check out the state nursery. They might give you some for this kind of project."

"Thanks, I will."

"Mayor, have you heard any rumbling from your folks about this project?"

"None I know of. Should I have?"

"I hear some folks are planning to come to see you and complain about these folks getting so much attention while some of your other neighborhoods need a little help."

"Where does that come from?"

"Don't know. Probably from some of the same folks we thought might have burned down the church. You know what I mean?"

"Thanks, I'll call Louise Edwards to see if she has heard much." "Any suggestions other than that?" "Naw, just mind your backside." "I will."

"Louise, this is Randy."

"I was out to Pleasant Hill this morning with Judge Leach and he has heard rumors that we may have some trouble about the clean up."

"Why didn't you tell me?"

Louise Edwards was a large woman with a henpecked husband and grown children. She had come on the scene in 1933 and was very skillful in manipulating the members of the council. She had a sincere interest in education and of all things, city planning. Fort Anthony did not have a planner on staff but they would soon if "Lady" Edwards had her way.

"Well, I have been trying to catch up around the bank and have gotten behind a little on local politics."

"Vern told me he was going to deal with Red and his bunch."

"They think it will raise their taxes?"

"Well, we need to tell them that almost no city money is being spent."

"Okay, what are they going to do?"

"Whaddaya mean, boycott the bank?"

"Dangit, Louise, I can't afford that!"

"I don't mind having a public hearing but we can't stop now. Don't they know this is good project and it will make us look good across the state? The Governor is in support; Ed Roundtree has gotten us some Roosevelt Money; Judge Leach is helping and well, crap, Louise, we don't need this right now!"

"What are they upset with Trotman about? The Governor told him to find the guy a house either on the campus or nearby."

"Fred told me that he got the guy a house on campus!"

"I'll call him. Yeah, talk to you later."

"Yeah, Randy." It was Dr. Trotman.

"Well, the guy who is living in the place decided not to leave."

"I can't fire him just to get a house for some other faculty member."

"It's a couple of blocks from the campus."

"I heard that neighborhood was not too happy."

"Okay, I'll tell the real estate agent to look closer for a rental house."

"They can't boycott the bank. Isn't that against the law?"

"When is the public hearing?"

"Okay, let me know."

"This is Reverend Shipley."

"Yes, Randy."

"No, I was not aware of any unrest."

"No, I did not reach Brother Lott."

"Well, Randy he is not easy to deal with."

"What would you have me do?"

"Let me pray about it."

"Randy, don't swear at me!"

"Yes, I'll work on it."

"Reverend Bartley, Please."

"Jim, this is Vern Shipley."

"I was doing great until Randy Roberts just called. He is very upset."

"It seems that he had a meeting with Judge Leach this morning over at Pleasant Hill to bring him up to date on the Neighborhood Improvement Project. He heard from the Judge that there is a sort of uprising about the work that is going on over there. He also heard that the neighbors around the college are upset because Fred is attempting to find a house for Ez Temple and his family off the campus."

"He said I had assured him that I could handle Reverend Joe Lott and his congregation."

"Well, I talked to a member over there who said that Joe is really mad at me for starting this."

"I know, I know; I hoped against hope that we would not have to face this kind of thing."

"Yes, our "good neighbor" sermons did not reach Red. One of his congregants told me that Red said to him once that he couldn't love a neighbor across the street unless he knew if he was lovable or not, much less one on Nigger Hill."

"Would you? That would help me a lot. Yes, if you will soften him up for me then I can follow up. Good; good, thanks Jim, I owe you one."

"Randy, Jim Bartley at 1st Pres is going to talk to Red."

"He said he would call me back ASAP."

"Okay."

"Roberta, set up a staff meeting late this afternoon."

"Rose, I may be late for dinner. I have a late meeting here at the bank."

"Fred, can you be over here at the bank for a meeting about 4:30?

It's a staff meeting but I need another director of the bank present."

"Louise, have you thought anymore about that public hearing?"

"Is that the soonest we can arrange it?"

"Okay, thanks."

Chapter Fifty-Eight

Real Estate Problems
The Evening of May 1, 1935

"Those colored people are already beginning to cause me trouble," fumed Randolph Roberts.

"What have they done?" asked Rose.

"All that trouble we have gone to for them: bringing them into the city, paving their street, spiffing up their park, marking their graves, paying their hospital bills, Fred getting that guy a house."

"What kind of trouble are you referring to, Randy?"

"Leach told me that trouble was brewing and I checked with Louise Edwards and she confirmed it."

"What kind of trouble are the colored folks causing you?"

"It seems that some of the old Fort Anthony taxpayers are upset."

"But what are the colored folks doing to cause you trouble?" Rose feigned perplexity.

"Some folks are talking about boycotting the bank."

"The colored folks?" More perplexed.

"No, but some of the people over near the college are upset that Fred is looking for a house for Ez Temple off the campus."

"Some of the colored folks are upset?"

"No, some of the neighbors over near the school."

"Randy I'm truly confused. You said that the colored folks are beginning to cause you trouble, but you haven't said a thing that the colored folks are doing."

"A lot of voters are mad because we annexed that neighborhood and fixed the road and plan to build a shelter in the park and put a fence around the graveyard."

"Colored voters?"

"And some say we must have a public hearing and they want to stop the project because it is going to cost a lot of city tax money."

"Some of the colored folks?" She wanted to pin him down.

"No, heck no. They haven't said a dang thing."

Catching Randy completely off guard, Rose asked, "Are you sure, they wanted to be annexed, or have the road fixed, or build a park, mark the graves, or put a fence around the old graveyard? Did any body ask them? Did Ez ask Fred to get him a house on or off the campus for that matter?"

Looking away, Randy said, "I guess not. But it is the right thing to do."

"Who says?"

"A lot of people."

"Do any of them pay property taxes in Collier County?"

"Heck, I don't know, but I can't have that bunch of rednecks boycotting the bank or ruining this city. They don't know a bulls-ass from a bass fiddle when it comes to running a city or a bank. I am fed up with that dang Red Lott and that bunch of Kluxers he's got up at that church of his. They can go to the dickens."

"Do they vote and pay taxes?"

"I guess so." Showing his frustration.

"Can I fix you a scotch and water?"

With relief, "Please."

Thursday morning on his walk to the bank, Randy noticed some spring flowers in bloom and ladies working in their gardens. A month or more into spring, yet he had not played golf or gone fishing or even taken a bike ride. He knew he should be out getting some exercise or going down to their lake house for some relaxation. He was tense and a little depressed. His back was beginning to bother him and he had extended his belt another notch. This is not what he had planned for this spring.

He had three scotches last night and had not slept well; never did after drinking too much. Rose was looking prettier than ever. He was very proud of her and looked forward to the baby they expected in November. She had pinned him to the wall about his complaints of trouble with the colored citizens-in a nice way of course. She was very good in intellectual discourse, but he must get accustomed to her direct responses.

Chapter Fifty-Nine

More Politics
Thursday Morning, May 2, 1935

"Hello, Louise, Randy here."

"I hope you can follow up on our conversation about a public meeting to go over the plans you have made for Pleasant Hill."

Randy's words tumbled out, "Well, I think that some charts with figures that show where the money is coming from. You know Federal money for the park, county inmates for the cleanup, state help on the road, the contribution of materials for the road from Beckham and Fils, and Mr. Beckham is sending the stone for the cemetery fence and the fireplace on the park shelter. We haven't anticipated any city expense have we?"

"The state is helping because the governor told them to!"

"The oversight can't be much can it?"

"Why don't I see if the bank won't pick up the cost of a clerk of the works? Those guys only make a couple of bucks a day."

Addressing the positive side of the project, Randy pointed out to the Vice Mayor, "Yeah, then we pick up some property that is subject to property taxes."

"I know it's not much but it will be something."

"Yes, the property owners will have to pay city and county property taxes. Hadn't thought much about that."

They both realized that the property owners on Hardscuffle

were not the residents!

"They will be receiving city police and fire protection. And soon we can run a city water line out there."

"I suppose you better put that on a chart, but let's show that as a possibility along with sewers and street lights."

"Thanks greatly. Will you call the city clerk's office and arrange for legal notice in the paper?"

"Good, let me know how I can help. Good-bye."

"President Trotman, please."

"Fred, what do you think of the staff meeting yesterday?"

"Sure, why don't I get that information and I'll come by your office after Rotary Club. Are you going?"

"It's a pretty day and I'm on foot too, so we can walk back to your place and review the numbers."

At the staff meeting on Wednesday afternoon, he had queried the employees about any rumors or clues they might notice of depositors removing funds or any organized effort to cause trouble for the bank. His bank was the only one in Fort Anthony to survive the crash and he would prefer to avoid much competition for as long as possible. If his political opposition had any ideas about seeking a new bank charter for Fort Anthony, he would hear from the Banking Commission in Indiana but he must keep a close eye on any movement in that direction.

The tellers and the cashier reported that there had been no unusual movement, but just in case, he asked for data on recent account withdrawals and closures. The Fort Anthony Bank made small personal loans and some auto loans, as well as all the commercial loans made to the businesses in the city. They had deposits from the college, all the churches, all the businesses, and about 60 percent of all other deposits. Some folks who had relocated here from towns nearby still maintained their savings accounts in a bank "at home" in order to maintain connections in case they moved back. Randy had encouraged these new residents to put their savings and checking at the same bank. However, it was obvious he still had work to do.

The Rotary Club consisted of about fifty of the top businessmen, professional men and clergymen in Fort Anthony. This all-male group met weekly to sing a song or two, eat a little lunch, gossip some and hear a program designed to enlighten them as to important matters going on in the world. No women and no colored folk. Their program was on "The Impact of the Roosevelt Administration on the Social Mores of Indiana Culture." A Professor of Political Science and Economics at the State College gave the address; it was a warmed over version of a paper he had given at The Indiana Association of Political Science Educators. Although it contained some helpful material, the presentation was less than sparkling. Some of the older members dozed.

Randy was interested in any gossip he might pick up concerning the annexation of the new territory by the city. Fred was listening as well, but his mind drifted off to his search for housing for Ez Temple.

On the walk to Fred's office Randy asked him, "Where did you get such a terrible speaker?"

"I wouldn't call him terrible, Randy."

"Sorry, I was impolite. Are all Teachers College teachers so boring?"

"Randy, these people are dedicated to what they do. However, if they were spectacular teachers, they would not be here in the first place. They would be at IU or some Ivy League school. Do you know what we pay a Ph.D. like him? It is pathetic! Unless we begin to understand that the teachers we put on the street are molding the future of our nation we will be in trouble. The future of our culture is at stake. You can bet on it."

"I guess that's what we're doing, aren't we?'

"You got it."

In Fred's office, the subject changed. Randy laid out the information he had assembled. In sixty days the bank had lost a net of thirty-five savings accounts. Forty were closed and five new ones opened. Twenty-two personal loans have been paid off and car loans were down by 18 percent. Two churches had closed both checking and savings and six small businesses had closed accounts. State government deposits were stable. So was the college account. Banks in the region were all paying the same three-percent on savings and charging from six to nine percent on loans.

"Something is going on, Randy!"

"I agree. I need to find if it is organized or what."

"Should you report this to the board?"

"I'll have to sooner or later. But whatever I tell them will need to be complete and based on good research."

From time to time, the bank had used a former newspaper reporter to investigate image problems and suggest ways to clear up such things. Randy thought that perhaps he would be good to help with this situation.

"Ed Negley, please."

Chapter Sixty

Public Relations
Thursday, May 2, 1935

Ed Negley was a hard-core investigative reporter of the old school if you did not get the dirt, you did not get the story.

He was half con-man and half adventure-writer. He had never won any awards but sold millions of papers. He had the face and build of a greyhound, but his nose for information was from a hound of a different breed. Negley had a slight mustache, an abundant head of grey hair and the trim muscled body of a marathon runner. His nickname was "Skinny" and he lived up to it.

These days he turned his talents to trouble shooting for troubled businesses. He could work as an undercover insurance investigator, as a bank teller or as a vice president with equal believability. His ability to worm a story out of the most reluctant politician was his trademark. Negley could sweet-talk a bear from his lair and get his life story. Randy knew him from a previous assignment-a touchy one calling for Negley's best-and had great confidence in him for this job.

"Mr. Mayor, how are you? Are you having fun yet?"

"Is this one of those times?"

"What's your problem?"

"So you want to find out who or what is behind all this boycott talk?"

"What I think doesn't matter. I need to turn over some rocks and find out what's what. Suppose we find out that Red what's his name is a Kluxer and that all the rednecks in the county do not want to do business with your bank. What in the name of peace can you do about it?"

"Okay, Randy, I'll get you some answers. Who's paying?"

"How much?"

"What's it worth?"

"You frigging skinflint you want me to pull your bank and your fat ass out of a ditch for twenty—five lousy bucks a week! Heckfire, I can get that working for the CWA!"

"Okay."

"Monday soon enough?"

"Get me a room."

"Not exactly a bright idea if you want to do some undercover investigation. Get me a room. Put it on my expense account."

"I'm easy. How much can I spend in that hick town of yours? I will keep track of the expenses with no padding, okay."

Chapter Sixty-One

The Klan is Alive and Well in Our Town
Thursday Morning, May 9, 1935

Ed had some information for Randy. Although he knew it would be better to tell him in person, he felt it important for Randy to be updated.

"Randy, I have got something for you. But you are not gonna like it. The bank is the subject of a Klan Boycott."

"When I started nosing around some of my old contacts when the Klan ran Indiana, that's what they say is going on now!"

"You wish. Remember when every elected county official across Indiana and the America Legion, the Republican Party and some religious groups were heavy into the Klan stuff? It is still true in some quarters. I read of a funeral recently where the old lady was buried in her Klan paraphernalia. I know you and your family are all church-going folks, Randy, but you cannot even imagine some of the old hatreds out there. It is left over from all the emigration following the war when the Catholics, Jews, Europeans and Middle Easterners came to this country in droves. Opening little grocery stores, small businesses and competing in the job market. The natives got restless and I'm not at all surprised at another example of that old fear. The word is that you and your white political cronies have teamed up with some coloreds and your bank is getting the fallout."

"Randy it doesn't matter what you are trying to make Fort Anthony.

Some folk's idea of a good place is different from yours and mine!"

"Randy it doesn't help to lose you temper. They can also break your bank!"

"Now just cool off. You have to play this thing right. That's why you called me. Before you do anything let me drive over there and we'll see what we can see."

Chapter Sixty-Two

The Power of Prayer
Monday Evening, May 13, 1935

"How was your drive down?"

"Thank God for paved roads. I can remember when most of the roads down here were tar and gravel."

"It's a fine thing too. I passed a lot of freight trucks on the road the last times I drove to Chicago."

"Have you lost anymore accounts since we talked?"

"One of the porters here at the bank said the colored Baptist preacher prayed for me and my family on Sunday. You know they pray for any and everything, but I never heard of them praying for a white family before. You know we have been trying to make things better for the coloreds and it may have been a coincidence. He thought it was a good thing for them to do but he seemed to think it was special. Haven't lost any more accounts though."

"I think I need to hear the whole story from asshole to elbow."

"C'mon we'll go over to the office. We can talk uninterrupted for as long as we need."

It was a pleasant late spring evening and they considered walking but Ed suggested they drive and park at the back and go in the conference room for their visit.

Ed asked Randy to start from the beginning, but he had a hard time identifying the genesis of the story. That is because he did not know when it all began. He did remember that a young colored boy had come to work for his uncle over at his Baptist church and he had been invited to a party for the emerging town symphony.

Under Ed's persistent queries; it came to him like an avalanche. It was almost as if Ed was a student of Dr. S. Freud and was psychoanalyzing him. Ed uncovered most of the story although it took him most all of the night and they were both exhausted.

"Where in heavens name have you been? You said you would be back in a couple of hours. Have you and Ed been over drinking at the club?"

"Sorry, I should have called. Ed has been cross-examining me for almost eight hours and I am beat. I need some rest."

"Cross-examining you? About what?"

"It's business. He is a community relations guy, ex-newsman who is going to help us with a new way to increase the profits of the bank. Now can I get some rest?"

"No, I'm tired too. I have been waiting up for you and I want to know what is going on. You have been moping around here like a puny pup, I want to help. If you are ill, I want to help. If you have a troublesome girlfriend and cannot get rid of her, I want to help. If it is bank business, I want to help. If it about something in the Mayors office, I want to help. We do not need all that political crap anyway. Now tell me what has got your nose in a twist."

"I'm not ready to talk about it. Can it wait until in the morning? I am really tired and my mind is dull as a rusty saw."

Chapter Sixty-Three

The Conspiracy
Tuesday, May 14, 1935

Randy awoke and Rose was gone. He was greatly relieved. He showered, dressed and called Ed Negley. There was no answer in his room at the hotel.

"I suppose he is having breakfast," Randy said to himself.

Randy drove to the coffee shop of the Wayne Anthony Hotel and went in to find Ed. He was surprised to see him sitting in a corner talking to Rose.

"Well Ed, is Rosie bending your ear about our late night carousing? Have you told her about that blonde goddess I introduced to you? What about all the Manhattans Raymond served us at the club?"

"No Randy, we have been talking about your soon to be heir and about your state of mind. Rose wants to be helpful."

Randy stood as straight as a pool cue and said to his wife, "Rose, would you run me back to the house I forgot something I will need today. Ed, you take my car and meet me at the bank." He dabbed at his eyes with his handkerchief.

Rose drove him home.

Ed went to the house by another route in Randy's car and arrived before the other two. He was waiting when they arrived.

Mary Ella prepared some sassafras tea while the three found comfortable seats in the parlor. She was told nothing to explain why they were here.

Ed asked Rose to give him a few minutes with Randy, alone. She reluctantly agreed. She went up to her bedroom and began to cry. It was an emotional moment for her but therapeutic. When Ed came up to talk to her she was ready to hear him out.

"Has he had a nervous breakdown?" she asked.

"Maybe, but he needs some rest for sure. How long has it been since you two relaxed somewhere together?"

"I suppose when we went to Chicago," she responded.

"Let's think this through: How about a trip to Lake Geneva till next Monday or Tuesday? That is not too long and you can say that you need some time together before the baby comes. I will arrange for a car and driver to meet us outside of town and shuffle the two of you off for a short respite. Remember this is for him to get away from his problems; whatever they may be. I will tell you what you need to know and no more. You must lay off questioning him and hope he can revive his spirit. He is a good man Rosie, and you are a fine couple. He just needs a break."

"What's the problem?" she asked pointedly.

"Some mysterious things have been going on at the bank and I am doing some research. I have not decided whether it is an inside job or somebody on the outside. Clearly, it could be either one. We are both treating this as a potential case for a grand jury and we must keep it between the two of us. I hope you understand."

Rose read between the lines but was still perplexed. She decided she would play along for the time being.

"Are you a lawyer? I thought you were a 'community relations consultant.' Sounds like he needs a lawyer."

"I do investigative work for lawyers as well as private businesses. I help them plan tactical moves and develop long-range strategies to solve problems. This thing is no big deal but he has a lot of pressure on him now. He has brought much of it on himself because he is such a caring person who loves this town. He is too nice for his own good! They say that no good deed goes unpunished and he is a doer of good deeds. I know it is not fair but that's life. He will be fine but he needs no pressure and your undivided, loving attention for the next few days."

Chapter Sixty-Four

Off to Lake Geneva
Tuesday Afternoon, May 14, 1935

Rose packed a few sweaters and some easy-to-wear resort clothes for the trip. It would be cool in Lake Geneva and they would need some warm things. Randy did not take his golf clubs but did pack his shoes, just in case. He could always rent clubs from the pro. He did call the pro at The Wabash Country Club to let the pro in Lake Geneva know that he would be in town for a long weekend and he would appreciate courtesy privileges.

Ed went to the train station about five that afternoon and transferred their luggage to the dark green La Salle sedan. However, the driver picked them up at the front door of the bank and they drove off for a little time for themselves. The cover story was that he had a meeting with the financial company for whom they were the local correspondent bank. Rose was invited and because of her condition, she did not want to take the night train to Chicago as Randy had planned.

Ed had arranged a leisurely trip. The driver took them over into Illinois and up State Route 1 to Danville where they stopped in for the night. He had arranged for the dinner stop outside town and then on to the railroad hotel for the night. It was clean but not fancy. The driver stayed in similar accommodations.

On Wednesday morning, they had a good breakfast of oatmeal, fried side meat and eggs with biscuits and plenty of butter, honey and jam.

Fortified for the day they headed north missing as many small towns as they could and arrived in Lake Geneva sometime after noon.

The driver left them at the resort and drove back to Chicago, his home base. Ed knew his stuff and the couple were happy for the time together.

Although the trip was a last minute thing, it was not unusual for Randy to go to Chicago for the day. The unusual part was his taking Rose and going up to Lake Geneva afterwards.

The other officers were surprised when Ed appeared at the hastily called meeting arranged by Roberta Cummins, Assistant to the President and long time gatekeeper for the various bankers who needed her help from time to time. She was sweet as molasses but tough to get past when the need arose.

Roberta introduced Ed to the senior loan officer and tellers. She explained he was a community consultant who worked with businesses to develop strategies for success and that he would like to visit with each of them. She made clear that he would be in town for about a week.

He told them that when he told his old friend Randy Roberts he would take the proposed assignment on condition that he could undertake it without notice and he would prefer that Randy be out of town. The study was to be confidential and the product of his work was designed to strengthen the bank in times like this present economic climate. He and Randy had planned the study for some time, but his work schedule was such that this was the time available and he would be as little trouble to them as possible.

"Why did you want Randy to be out when you were here?" asked a cashier.

"Good question. Thank you for asking. I did not want anyone to seek Randy's advice about what to tell me when we talk. He wants you to give straight answers and not be influenced by his presence. When I leave next week, I doubt if you will ever see me again. Nothing you tell me will be attributed to you or you or you. We are working in confidence on both sides of the deal. My proposals will be based on the facts I see on the ground here and in the community. Mr. Roberts is the single most dedicated citizen of this town and a fine banker! He wants what is best for the stokeholders of this bank, for the people who work here and for the entire community."

Roberta, a strong presence among her peers, stood up, thanked them for coming and called on the participants to cooperate in every way possible. "Now let's go back to work."

Ed thought to himself that she might be the best asset and friend Randy has in this place.

Meanwhile, back at Lake Geneva, Randy and Rose were napping after a late lunch with one martini for Randy and a glass of white wine for Rose. They needed this.

Chapter Sixty-Five

Getting Down to Business
Noon Wednesday, May 15, 1935

Roberta ordered a box lunch for Ed and herself so that they could discuss the next steps.

When Roberta came in the conference room with a crystal pitcher and some tumblers with ice, Ed stood, saluted, and told her how appreciative he was for her support. "I know it was unplanned but that is how I work best," he told her. He offered profuse thanks to her and told her how much Randy would appreciate her help in this time.

She asked what she could do to help.

As they began to eat the sliced chicken sandwich from the "Get Along Go Along Tea Room," he told her he had several lists with which he needed her input.

Who are they and where do they bank:

- Ethnic communities and the leadership
- Churches and the leadership-both the hired help, length of tenure and the lay leaders
- Business leaders
- Daily newspapers
- Radio stations that serve this region
- Farm equipment and truck dealers
- Grange, Elks, Eagles, American Legion Posts, Masonic leaders
- Feed and Seed store

- Farm supply stores
- Stock yards
- The Volunteer Fire Department

He would like to meet as many key players as possible, but he would also like to meet many common folk.

Roberta told Ed that there were not any common people in Fort Anthony. She had a little grin on her face that he noticed often. She was a pleasant enough person and he might take her out to lunch soon.

While Ed was riding around the countryside to get his bearings and become familiar with landmarks and the rural road system, Roberta and the cashier Sam Huntley were hard at it.

When he returned after his travels around the district, he found Roberta and Sam still at work in the conference room making lists with key players, addresses, and other pertinent info.

"You are really as Randy described to me: Fine bankers and dedicated staff. Let's eat supper. We can go to the club where we can have a drink and relax."

Chapter Sixty-Six

Long Distance and More Business
Early Friday Morning, May 17, 1935

Randy put in an early call to Roberta Cummins at her apartment over Abe Shunarah's Dry Goods Store.

"Good morning Mr. Roberts."

"Not really, Mr. Roberts."

"No calls that can't wait."

"Fine, how are you feeling?"

"And Rose?"

"Need anything special or just checking in?"

"When are you coming back?"

"No—you?"

"Call anytime."

"Who was that?"

"Randy."

"You didn't tell him I was over here, did ya?"

"Not a chance, he thinks I'm an old maid and set in my ways. You can hang around but I need to go to work."

"Me too, I'll get a shower if you don't mind. I've got some calls to make."

"Make yourself at home."

"Thanks, I'll see you later. It was nice."

"Think so?"

"You didn't think so?"

"I'll buy lunch. Meet me at the *Noodle Nook* about 12:15 for a bowl of soup and a sandwich. See ya?"

"Sure."

Sam skipped supper with them, worked late, and came up with 103 retail stores, food markets, gas stations, insurance agents, government offices, farm supply stores, tractor and equipment companies, a couple of dairies, drug stores, cafes, roadhouses, soft drink distributors, a small bottling company, two small canneries, two small-parts factories and other assorted enterprises. The agriculture list included 73 grain farms and 15 truck gardens, 10 hog farmers, 4 chicken farms, 5 sawmills and two plant nurseries.

Roberta took a hiatus for some supper and relaxation from the research but identified: 2 cemeteries, 3 funeral homes, 1 radio station, 1 newspaper, 23 churches, 14 social service agencies, 5 ag societies including the 4-H and FFA counselors, 2 political societies, the library guild, 6 garden clubs, the volunteer fire hall, 4 civic clubs, 1 Klavern, The Knights of Columbus, The Masons, the Eagles, the Elks, and the Grange. All with bank accounts or cash in hand that ought to be in somebody's bank!

Sam had a good Remington typewriter and Roberta had a new Royal. They each typed up their own list but according to Sam's directions.

Meanwhile, Ed was on the road stopping at stores, roadhouses, soda fountains, barbershops (a trim in one and shave in the other) the newspaper (*The Weekly Indianan*) and the radio station (WFAI-760) to chew the fat. *The Guardian* was on the streets on Thursday and the station was picking up the latest farm reports from Chicago prior to some local programming. The Farm and Home Hour would be on shortly so the station/announcer/salesman/engineer could chat for a few minutes. Ed went to the soda fountain downstairs, bought two large root beers and a tuna salad sandwich for his host to eat while they visited.

Ed, ever the reporter, picked the brain of the radioman like feathers off a scalded chicken. It was no match.

Chapter Sixty-Seven

The Queen of Gossip
Friday, May 17, 1935

At the bank, it had been an interesting Friday morning. Etta Rains stopped by early to see Roberta and gossip for about ten minutes during which time, she asked about Randy and the expectant Rosie and who was that fellow with her at the club last night?

"Sam told me he was a 'community consultant' for the bank—what is a 'community consultant?'"

Roberta, ever calm, was flustered and surprised at how much she knew. Etta, who was approximately Roberta's age, wrote the society column for *The Indianan*, edited the letters to the editor and did two radio shows. Her Society column featured the gossip that she regurgitated on her Friday morning radio show. On Saturday morning, she took the calls for the "Swap and Shop" segment where she also mixed local chatter to create interest for the listeners. Although, she was sponsored by the bank on Saturday mornings, she was not to be trusted.

Roberta was a staunch Methodist and had no time for that bunch of Stoneite "Disciples" where Etta went to church. Many of them were mixed up with the Klan and her preacher was the Klavern Kludd. He was thought to be a personal friend of D. C. Stephenson, the Republican politician and Klan leader who scandalized the whole Midwest several years ago. She did not know if Etta had been a Klan member but it was not unusual for many of Indiana's leading citizens to be deeply involved in the Klan back then.

Roberta took a deep breath and spoke quietly.

"Randy and Rose are fine. She went to Chicago with him on a business trip, and they went up to Lake Geneva for some relaxation before the baby arrives. Sam told you right. Mr. Negley is a consultant Randy engaged to offer ways the bank can serve this community better. Mr. Negley asked me to join him at the club so we could discuss his project."

"I heard you were drinking hard liquor with him."

"For your information I had lemonade and Mr. Negley had a Manhattan. We talked business and went home early."

Roberta regretted her tone of voice immediately. "Etta, I did not mean to sound short with you, but Sam and I are responsible for the bank in Randy's absence and I'm covered up. Let's have a cup of tea together soon and we can have a good conversation then."

"Would you excuse me I need to go into a small staff meeting?"

Etta had developed a keen ear for voice inflections, nervousness and guilt. She thought to herself, "Hmmm, why isn't Randy here while his 'consultant' is in town? Did Roberta have gin in her lemonade? Why wasn't the 'consultant' at the hotel coffee shop this morning like he has been since he got here?"

Roberta stopped by Sam's window and asked him to join her in Randy's office.

"Sam, what in the name of heaven were you doing talking to Etta Rains? No telling what she will spread around town!"

"Crap, Roberta, I—"

"Don't you swear at me?"

"I wasn't swearing at you!"

"Okay, forget it. What did you tell her?"

"I saw her on the sidewalk late yesterday afternoon as I was walking home and she asked me what was going on. She is a customer at the bank for Gods sake! We sponsor her radio show, and she is a good Christian woman. I didn't do nothing wrong! Why don't you get off my back? I am not some snotty-nosed kid who got into town last night on a turnip truck. I am a professional banker; I will be president of a bank someday! That's more than you can say. You're just a dang secretary! Who are you to go around questioning me! I worked hard to get up all that information for your boyfriend—"

"Wait a minute you shrimp, He's not my boyfriend, I hardly even know the man."

"I saw the way you look at him. What's a dried up old maid like you carrying on like a 10th grader?"

Roberta realized she had lost her temper with Sam and apologized. "Okay, Sam, I'm sorry I jumped to the wrong conclusion. I'm just a little on edge while Mr. Roberts is away. Just forget it but let's not say anything to anybody until Mr. Roberts gets back. He will know how to handle this." She offered her hand in truce, but he turned and walked back to his cage.

While Ed was at the radio station, he could hear what was going on in the studio. A small speaker was fitted into the ceiling in the hallway where they were sitting. He heard a female voice doing her chatty community roundup show. "Not unusual," he thought until he heard the words "the Roberts," "Community Consultant," and "Girl Friday Roberta."

Ed asked, "Who is your on-air personality now? Sounds interesting. She could be helpful in my research."

"Would you like to meet her?" Under his breath, he said to Ed, "She's just a gossip and a troublemaker. But she is a good friend with our station owner and likes to be behind a mike spreading her meaness around. She has many women listeners and they hear her on Saturday morning on her swap and shop show. She's just another female gossip. They will be cluttering up the airwaves one of these days."

Ed wondered if he should hang around and meet her or head to lunch with Roberta. "I wish I could but I have an appointment shortly. Thanks for your time. I am sure you can help the bank help this community."

"That's why we're here."

He was off to join Roberta for lunch at the "Noodle Nook."

Chapter Sixty-Eight

A Homegrown Run
Friday, May 17, 1935

The tearoom was right around the corner from the bank but a good way from the radio station. Ed was in good condition, considering his sedentary profession. He only drank liquor in the company of others and smoked a social cigar now and again. Ed was a vegetarian but ate fish from the local waters. He generally stayed away from sodas because of the reputation it had earned when it was made with cocaine and he walked at least a mile a day. For 57 he was the picture of health.

Roberta recently had her "Golden Birthday." Nifty fifty was not so bad she thought with fond memories of the previous night's adventure. She was almost as tall as Ed and watched her weight. Never married, her career was all she had time for, she told herself. She had allowed herself a couple of flings when she went up to Chicago or to New York for ABA meetings. Bankers were not very inventive lovers she thought. Sam Huntley was typical of the stodgy, cigar smoking, pot-bellied bankers she knew. Mr. Roberts was atypical and she envied Rose for her relationship with a man she worshipped. He was a good bit her junior ,but she was attracted to him. She knew it was not to be and she kept her cards breasted at all times.

"You're late," she smilingly scolded him as he slid into the booth beside her. "Don't you think you had better sit across from me?"

He quickly moved when he noted the worried look on her face.

"Something wrong?"

Her eyes were moist when she said, "I have had a hard morning."

An hour later, after a couple of BLT's and two glasses of iced raspberry tea, she finished her story. Ed suggested they go over to the hotel restaurant for a cup of strong coffee and a piece of egg custard pie. They chose a corner table, ordered the egg custard pie and he told her of his visit to the station.

Back at the bank, Sam was nervous as a cat on a hot barn roof. Two women came to cash out their accounts and were not too friendly. The treasurer of the Stoneite church had done the same thing. It was getting on towards two o'clock and Roberta was not back from lunch. The bank closed at three on Friday so he thought nothing bad could happen between now and three.

Chapter Sixty-Nine

A Short Stop
Friday, May 17, 1935

"I had better get back to the bank. We close in a little more than an hour and there is no telling what Sam has stirred up."

"I'll appear before three and we can all have a little talk."

Ed walked to his car and disappeared.

Roberta walked back to the bank.

Sam was busy as a frog in a frying pan. There were ten women at his window shouting and clamoring to get the attention of the cashier. He was trying to be calm but it was hard to do.

Roberta walked over to the group at Sam's window and asked if she could help.

"Yeah, gimme my money. You've got ninety five dollars in that safe over there that belongs to me and I want it."

"I want my forty four bucks! Here's my savings book."

"Where is Mr. Roberts? Etta Rains told me he has mysteriously left town with Rose in the middle of the night and I want my money, now."

"Hold on Ladies. Mr. Roberts needed to go to a bankers' meeting in Chicago and he took Rose with him so they could take a few days off before the baby comes. All of you mothers know what it means to be relaxed when that happens."

"When is the baby due?"

"I honestly don't know. All I know is they both needed some rest and he thought this would be a good time to get it."

"You know 'ever' thing else about him. You ought to know when her baby is due!"

"Okay, friends this is not a big deal. We have your money in the safe and you can get it out right now. It just takes a little time to close out an account. Everybody be calm please and I will tend to it immediately!"

Roberta moved behind the cage and told Sam to get all the cash in all the tellers' cages and from the safe. He piled it up next to the deal plate in his cage and she would help these good folks. Sam stood on a wooden cold drink case and she did as well. The taller the better she thought.

"Now ladies," she spoke in a tone as cool as a cucumber, "let's get down to business."

"Ladies here is over twenty thousand dollars! How much do you need?"

There was a unanimous sigh of relief.

"How much money is that again?" asked the church treasurer.

"Something over twenty thousand of good old Uncle Sam's bucks!"

"You keep that much money around here? Miss Etta said she thought you were broke."

"Well, I saw Sister Rains just this morning and she did not ask me about it. I wish she had: I would have shown her this pile of money as well if she wanted to see it."

The crowd of women simmered down but more kept coming in. There was a lot of chatter amongst them and the group slowly moved away from the cashiers cage.

One of the group, Sister Alpharetta Saine, confronted Roberta, "Sister Rains told me that Mr. Roberts was spending the bank's money helping those niggers with all those sidewalks and that damn park. What about that?"

"Randy Roberts is also Mayor of Fort Anthony. His job as Mayor is to see that all the citizens of our wonderful city have appropriate services on an equitable basis and he has asked for and received funds from the United States government and the President's wife Mrs. Roosevelt will be coming to Fort Anthony when the improvements are completed to cut the ribbon on the opening day."

"Well, that crazy nigger lovin' woman is a blight on this nation. I have heard she doesn't even go to church and doesn't believe in God. She must think she's God!"

"Mrs. Roosevelt is a loyal American woman and wonderful citizen who desires to see all our people prosper and live a good life in security and with hope!"

"Yeah, just like Mayor Roberts wanting to spend other peoples hard-earned money on these black-ass monkeys. I want my money now and I want to close my account and I am going to move it to a bank where people are 100 percent American, who don't even do business with Jews, Catholics and foreigners!"

"I'll be happy to accommodate you, Miss Alphie. How much is in your account? May I see your savings book?"

"Let's see that's thirty six dollars and sixty seven cents. Let me calculate the interest."

"That comes to thirty seven dollars and four cents. Would you like to have three tens and a five or all ones."

"Gimme all ones and four new pennies."

"Thank you Miss Alphie. Come in to see us anytime."

Alphie Saine stood at the cage and counted her ones and four pennies. "I said I wanted four new pennies. You gave me an old Indian Head penny."

Roberta had not noticed and gave her a shiny new penny. She put the Indian Head in a special place and would add it to her coin collection when she had a chance.

The crowd dispersed about the time that Ed appeared.

Roberta had paid out seven hundred forty seven dollars and eighty-five cents. Not bad for an attempted run on a little country bank, she thought. She smiled at Ed with relief as he approached her desk.

She instructed the tellers to tally up their business for the day.

"Ed tells me he has arranged for a private room at the hotel where we will have some hors-d'oeuvres and light refreshments for everybody. We can talk there and you can leave by four thirty."

Elder Ricketts witnessed the near debacle and stayed close to Roberta. She knew that he was there as a stand-in for the bank president. "Mr. Ricketts" Roberta gave him a hug. "Mr. Ricketts what would we do without you! Would you like to join us at the hotel for our meeting?"

"Oh no, Miss Roberta. They would make me come in the back door and will not even let me go in the Coffee Shop. It wouldn't be good for me to crash your party like that."

"Why that is absurd! We would love to have you and the hotel will let you in the front door when you show up with us."

"No ma'am. I need to go by the house and check on Miss Mary Ella to see if she is alright. This is not a good time to start something controversial with those Old Millenalites. They don't really like coloreds and we don't need to stir them up any more."

"You are right, I am sure. Here," she handed him a crisp new fifty-dollar bill, "Take off for a few days and come back on Wednesday when things will have cooled down."

"Oh, Miss Roberta, I've never seen a fifty dollar bill. That is too much. I can go to Chicago on that and have a big time for a week. Here take that back. Mr. Randy wouldn't like you to do that."

"Ed, Mr. Roberts loves you like a brother. There is nothing he would not do for you."

Tears came into Elder Ed Ricketts eyes. "I love him too. I love all my folks here at the bank. Thank you, Miss Roberta."

Roberta reflected on how much we depend on each other in the good times and the bad. Mr. Ricketts was someone you could count on.

"Now, Sam Huntley, don't feel bad. It could have happened to me. Come on and join us. I'll walk over with you."

Chapter Seventy

Honest Abe
Friday Afternoon, May 17, 1935

Ed Ricketts went directly to Abe Shunarrah's store on the square. "Come in Mr. Ricketts, How can I help you?"

"Mr. Abe I would like to buy a pair of those high-top lace-up shoes like you got on. How much are they?"

"Let's see Mr. Ricketts, these are made out of lambskin and they are pretty high."

"How high is that, Mr. Abe?"

"It's the best shoe I carry; they are easy on the feet and shine up real good. I sure would like to see you in a pair but they are $4.95 a pair."

"Have you got my size? I think I'm going over to Indianapolis to see my sister and go to church with her. I need a new shirt and one of those preacher ties. This old suit will have to do for right now."

Ed, "Sounds like you struck it rich. Have you been playing the numbers somewhere? Did your sister bet a dime for you?"

"Nosirree. They give me a little bonus over to the bank and Miss Roberta told me to take a little trip. So I'm going to Naptown for a few days. They are good folks over at that bank."

"Have you got $7.00, Mr. Ed."

"I've got fifty dollars. Most money I ever had at one time. Ain't that something?"

Abe Shunnarah was beside himself. "What size do you wear? Look like about a 10D and your shirt size looks to be around 15-15 1/2. Here try these shoes on and I'll get a shirt or two. Do you have any socks on? I'll throw in a pair of black ones with the shoes. Here ya go. How do they feel?"

"Best feeling shoe I ever wore."

"There, see what I told ya. Don't they feel great?" "Now try this shirt on. Arrow shirt, good as any man in town would have. How about this tie? Look good for Sunday. Is your sister a Baptist, too? Good folks you Baptists. I had an uncle who married a Baptist. Not many Baptists where I come from but he found one. Yessir, good folks you Baptists.

"You take these with you and if your sister don't like 'em you bring 'em right back next week.

"How about a spring hat. I got some new ones straight from Panama. Got a cousin down there who works in a factory that makes hats and he sends some special handmade ones just for spring up here to me. Just a buck for this new handmade Panama hat. I have a size 7 right here. No, looks like you need a 7 1/8. There now, you are ready to travel.

"How much is your bus ticket. Be sure and buy a roundtrip ticket. I wouldn't want one of my best customers to leave town and not come back. Here let me get a big shopping bag with handles for you. Do you have a suitcase? Here let me give you another one for your other things. I usually charge 10 cents each for those bags but that one is on the house.

"Miss Alphie ring up Mr. Ricketts. That will be 7.95 including the extra shopping bag. Mr. Ricketts is going on a trip to see his sister so he will need the extra bag."

"Hello, Ed—where did a nigger like you get a new fifty dollar bill? I was over at the bank a while ago and got some new pennies but no new bills. You must be in tight with those crooked bankers. I had to beat the door down to get my money out. Miss Etta Rains told me that Mr. Roberts has left town and the bank was broke. Hell, I got my money out quick. No bank will ever go broke on me again. I'm too smart."

"I don't know nothing about none of that. Miss Alphie I changed my mind. I don't think I need all this fine merchandise. Could I pay you for the socks and one of these bags?"

"Abe, come over here. This nigger has changed his mind and don't want his goods."

"Mr. Ricketts have you decided not to go to Indianapolis? I made you the best deal I could make you on that merchandise. What's the problem? Did I say something to make you unhappy? How about if I throw in the tie?"

"No sir, Mr. Abe. I just think I oughta shop some wheres else. Thank you for all your trouble. You are a good man."

Chapter Seventy-One

Going to "Naptown"
Friday Night 7:00 May 17, 1935

Ed Ricketts was at the bus station with a few things in his bag and a one-way ticket to Indianapolis. He decided that he could call back Monday and explain what had happened to Miss Roberta.

There was only one men's room at the bus station and he needed to stop in there before he took that long dark ride.

"What you doing in here, nigger? Don't you know only white men are supposed to use this privy?"

"Mister, I have a long way to travel this evenin and I need to use the toilet."

"Where you from, boy?"

"I live right here."

"Well, go home to do your business. Nobody wants to use a toilet after your black ass has set on it. Get the crabs or something. Now go on before I kick your ass out of here."

"Mister I can't make it back home and catch the bus to Indianapolis. Please sir, I won't be very long and I'll clean off the seat when I'm through."

With that, the thug slapped Elder Ricketts and knocked him up against a lavatory. Ed tried to stand but the thug hit him again.

"I'll teach you monkeys to crap in a white man's rest room. Now go out behind a tree and do your thing before I smack you again."

Another white patron came into the men's room about the time Ed was hit the first time. He retreated and called for the security to come help. The security man burst in the door and saw Ed attempting to stand and defend himself.

He hit Ed on the shoulder with his billy club and then took two shots to his head. Ed fell to the ground in a big black lump.

"Somebody call a doctor," the second patron shouted, "get the sheriff, somebody come in here and help this man, he's hurt bad."

"He ain't hurt. He's just playing possum. That is funny ain't it? A coon playing possum." The thug wasn't as sure as the security man who had delivered the severe blows.

"These coloreds come in this station and want to tell me how I should do my job. I'm here to keep the peace and by Gawd I am gonna do it! Ain't no coon playing possum gonna stop me!"

A crowd had gathered. The thug thought better of the situation and walked out of the bus station into the twilight never to be seen in these parts again.

The sheriff soon appeared with a city policeman to survey the scene. A nurse planning to catch the same bus as Ed came to help and said that Elder Ed Ricketts had no heartbeat.

Quiet ruled the waiting room in the small bus station. Interrupting the silence were whispers—"What happened?" "Is he really dead?" "What was a black man doing in that restroom anyway?" "Who is he?" "Worked at the Bank?"

"Oh, I know him. He is—was the porter at the Roberts's bank that Miss Etta was talking about on WFAI today. A real nice man, so polite, he wouldn't hurt a fly."

"What was Etta gossiping about today?"

"She declares their bank is in some kind of trouble."

"I don't believe a dang thing that gossipy old woman says. She has made more trouble for more folks than the law allows."

A hearse appeared on the street in front of the station to pick up the corpse. The two attendants took a stretcher into the rest room to collect the body.

"We don't haul niggers," said the driver.

"Gimme the keys to that truck you call a hearse. Set the stretcher down and the police officer and I will take care of this. Now get the hell out of here."

The sheriff recalled the lecture given by the Governor when the colored Baptist church was burned. He did not want the Governor on his butt.

By that time, the Police Chief had appeared with his only detective and an assistant district attorney.

"Chief, I locked this place down as soon as I could but I can't guarantee everybody is here that might have been involved. The station security officer is here and he can identify who else was in the rest room with him when this occurred."

"Good job, Tony, see if he can identify that person ASAP. Let the sheriff and a couple of our officers get this man on the stretcher and out of here. Do they not have a decent gurney to haul his body out? Does anyone know who he is? He kneeled down closer to the man and as he raised back up he said, "My God, this is Elder Ed Ricketts from out on Hardscuffle. He works for Randy Roberts at the bank and helps him out at his house as well. Who the hell would want to kill this man?"

The chief was enraged. "Take him out of here carefully and take him to Oakes Funeral Home. Tell them I said to keep this undercover, but to take care of him just like if he was my daddy!"

Meanwhile, the detective had begun questioning the small group left at the station. The security officer was told to sit down and shut up. The one observer of the crime scene could only be sure he saw the three men. The dead man, the security officer and another unidentified man. He was asked to come to the station and make a statement. He was on his way to Indianapolis but the Chief told him he would send him over in a patrol car if he missed the bus. He was a local man affiliated with the Ford dealership.

The security man was the former court officer for one of the judges impeached for involvement with the Klan eight years ago. He was hauled to the police station for a statement as well. The third man if such existed had disappeared.

The Police Chief asked his entourage "Who is going to call Mayor Roberts?" No response. "Guess it will be me."

A rookie cop offered this information, "I heard today on the radio that he was out of town for a long weekend."

"Is anybody at his house?" No response. "I had better ride by there."

When the chief pulled up to the house, it was well lighted. He went to the door to be met by Mary Ella who was sobbing. Roberta Cummins came to the door and welcomed him.

"You've heard?"

"Yes, what happened?"

"Some transient bum got in a fight with him at the men's restroom at the bus station."

"How do you know he was transient and a bum? Have you got him in custody?"

"No ma'am, I guess I just assumed he had gone into the restroom saw Mr. Ricketts in there and they had a fight. The security man at the station says that all he did was stop the fight."

Roberta inquired, "Where is the body?"

"Over at the Oakes place."

"Chief, call them right now and tell them not to touch the body. We will want to send the body to Chicago for an autopsy."

"Why not to Indianapolis?"

"Chief Mankiwitz, we will want the best possible investigation of this murder. If the county won't pick up the cost, the bank will. We have an investigator in town already looking into some other matters and he will oversee this situation for the bank."

"Are you going to call the Mayor?"

"Yes! I suggest you go back to the scene and I will have Mr. Ed Negley meet you. He may be there now."

Chapter Seventy-Two

The Bus Station
Friday Night, May 17, 1935

"Chief, I'm Ed Negley. I hope you will give Mayor Roberts and those of us at the bank the courtesy of allowing me to join you as you pursue justice in this tragic murder. We would be grateful if you will run any public comments by me."

"Miss Cummins will speak for the Roberts Family and the Bank. Mayor Roberts counted Elder Ricketts among his close friends and a highly trusted bank employee. Miss Cummins asked me to find out about Mr. Ricketts personal effects. He was planning a brief trip and he could have had some gifts for his sister or a fifty-dollar bill on him. Will you ask a member of your force to check that out ASAP?"

"Absolutely! Glad you reminded me. Jerry come over here a minute." The rookie jumped to and was at the chief's side.

"Jerry, have you located any of Elder Ricketts personal effects and did anyone look in his pockets."

"Yessir, I'll get on it now! Chief, somebody did tell me about a shopping bag from Abe Shunarah's store. I think it's over here inside the rest room. We have left the crime scene as it was. Nobody's touched nothing."

"Bring it here. We were in a hurry to get his body out of here," He said rather sheepishly. "Here we are. Take a look Mr. Neckley."

"The name is Negley."

"I'm sorry."

Ed thought, "I could believe that. But what can you expect in a small Indiana country town." He sorted through Mr. Ricketts meager travel wardrobe and toiletries and asked the Chief if he would have it inventoried on the spot so they could take it back to the station. "Would you call the station and ask them not to bother his clothing till I get there."

"Jerry, run over to the Oakes Funeral Home and tell them to leave the body and his personal effects alone. Mr. Negley will be there shortly."

Roberta was still wet-eyed when he arrived at the house. Mary Ella was resting but had prepared a pot of sassafras tea. The evening had turned coolish and the hot beverage hit the spot.

"Anything new?" Roberta asked.

"Not much. Have you called Randy?"

"I think it will be better in the morning."

"You are probably right. The money was not on him or in his poke. He was traveling light. He had purchased his ticket and it was in his shirt pocket. His head was beat on pretty bad. We have the billy that the house cop used on him. If I were a betting man, and I am, I'd lay 500 to 1 that dang houseman killed him. He says Ed was having a fight with some big white guy that he had never seen before and he was just trying to separate them. Said that Ricketts had a mean look in his eye when he walked in the toilet and was getting ready to hit this other man."

"The man who discovered the fight said that Mr. Ricketts was on the floor when he stuck his head in the door and the big white fellow was kicking him. Who would I believe the house cop or the bookkeeper at the Ford place?"

"The bookkeeper of course, but where did the other man go?"

"Disappeared into the sunset. Last time anybody saw him he was hightailing it on foot toward the river. No one could identify him or give much of a description to the city detective. We may never find him but I do not think he is the killer. They have locked up the other guy and charged him with criminal assault."

Chapter Seventy-Three

At the Police Station
Friday Night, May 17, 1935

Ed Negley spent most of the night at the police station while the detective was questioning the bus station guard.

The eye witness was placed in Chief Mankiewitz' office to be questioned by the Assistant DA who treated him with kid gloves. He was frightened and feared for his life.

The bookkeeper heard rumors about the antics of Hoosier politicians several years ago and when he learned that the security guard worked for a judge convicted of some kind of Klan connection he was tempted to flee the area just like the thug he saw manhandling the colored man.

His testimony at the station house was consistent with the report he gave on the scene. The stenographer brought in from the on-call list was instructed to keep everything confidential and to type the testimony immediately so the witness could sign it before leaving for Indianapolis. About 9:30, he was hustled to an unmarked city vehicle and driven to his destination as promised.

The guard's name was Alfred Newton Saine. He had come to Fort Anthony to play college basketball from Rockford High School in Illinois. He flunked out the first year and did odd jobs around town. He met and married Alpharetta Scott a couple of years later. He was known around town as Newt but some just called him "N." As a ball player, he was a roughneck on both the football field and the basketball court. He was 6'3" and played tackle on his high school football team and center on the basketball squad. He was well past his youthful prime at 185 and all muscle. At 290, his protruding belly fell over his belt and his shirttail hung out. He was considered a monster and the perfect match for his job of keeping the peace at the bus station. His only weapon was a large hickory billy club he carried with him constantly, almost seemed to be a natural extension of his still muscular right arm.

The Judge hired him for his reputation when he was still young and in fair shape. The Judge presided over the toughest cases in the county system. Newt was his shadow. Paid by the state, he was driver, personal bodyguard, valet on professional association trips and fellow Klansman.

When he worked for the Judge, he carried a Sheriff's Deputy Badge and a large S&W pearl handled revolver displayed prominently on his right hip. There were those who congregated in the courtroom just to watch "N" Saine. He put on a show and the judge loved it. They were a pair of rascals. The dysfunctional court officer and the crooked judge became well known throughout the area. Now they were both behind bars.

When he did not come home from the bus station after it closed at 8 o'clock, Alphie called Zoe's Village Inn where he had a beer or two every evening before supper. She had heard rumors about a fracas at the station and felt sure that Newt was involved. After all, he was there to protect the customers and it was natural he would be in the middle of everything.

"Has anybody over there seen Newt? I'm a little worried about him?"

"I know he can take care of himself. I just hope he is alright. Check it out."

"What is he at the police station about?"

"Well, why in the hell didn't you ask him?"

"Okay, I'll check over there?"

The preliminaries had been completed and the detective began the questioning of the suspect, Newt Saine, in a serious manner. Ed Negley could witness the process through a glass window between the chief's office and the interrogation room. The lights were turned off and Newt was unaware of the presence of a witness to the exchange.

The stenographer was available in case Newt wanted to make a notarized statement for the record.

In a calm voice, the chief queried the suspect, "Now Newt, we have known each other since you came to town. You were in the Judge's office when I was a rookie. But I have to put aside all that and do my job the best way I know how. I talked to the DA and he says he will give you a break if you cooperate."

Remaining calm, he told Newt, "The body is going to Chicago for an autopsy and if the death came as a result of blows to the head by your night stick you are facing a difficult time ahead."

"You can make it easy on yourself by telling me what happened and if you did hit Mr. Ricketts with your billy you can negotiate some kind of deal with him."

Newt growled, "How did you know I hit him with my stick?"

"Did you?"

"I never said I did or I didn't."

"Well, did you? Tell me now and I'll call in the DA and you can make a statement, he will take you before the Judge and maybe you can go home. By the way, Miss Alphie has been calling all over town looking for you. I heard she is on the way over."

Face down, Newt said, "I wish she would leave me alone."

"Now is a bad time to be alone, Newt. You are going to need all the help you can get."

Newt said, "Look this guy, you saw him, came out of the toilet and said there was fight going on. It's my job to keep peace and quiet at that place. I responded and pulled them apart. The nigger was fixing to hit that white guy and I couldn't get him off the white guy without using a little of my hickory persuader. I tried to hit him on his back and shoulders but he was so quick and fierce I may have put a lick on his head, I don't remember."

Chief Mankiewiez pressed him, "Newt if we must send that body to Chicago and the report from the medical examiner up there shows he died from blows to the head you could fry. If you tell me exactly what you did now, I will call in the district attorney and see what kind of deal you can make."

"Fry? Fry for what? I didn't mean to kill the guy. It was in the line of duty. I'm a law-abiding citizen and I am a peace officer. I'm not a murderer!"

"I know you say you are not the killer, but the circumstances all tell me you were doing your job and maybe you hit him too hard and they will take that into consideration. If you don't cooperate, they will bring up your record of barroom fights, that other assault arrest that the Judge threw out and the fact that you are a Klansman. You are still in the Klan aren't you?"

"How did you know that? Maybe I am and maybe I'm not. How you gonna find out?"

Mankiewiez reminded Newt of his past, "We got records of Klan activity for the last ten years. You and the Judge were both in the Klan together and although he is still in jail, he's still on the Roll of Honor of government officials of Indiana who were and are Klansmen. As a matter of fact we know that Miss Alphie is a member of the women's branch, or whatever they call it."

"I want to see her!"

Alphie was in the booking area and the sergeant escorted her to the interrogation room. The chief left the room and went into the his office.

"Whaddaya think Mr. Negley?"

"I wish that testimony was before the grand jury."

"The steno was taking notes."

"Where was she?"

"In a little nook I set up for just this purpose."

"Good thinking."

Dubious, Ed asked, "Is she still able to hear them?"

"Yep, it's all legal."

Ed said under his breath, "Maybe not ethical but legal, huh?"

Chapter Seventy-Four

At the Police Station
Friday Night, May 17, 1935

Quietly, an anguished Miss Alphie asked, "What happened?"

"Some nigger started a fight in the men's toilet and he died." A nervous Newt commanded, "Be quiet. They're probably listening. What'd he die of?"

"How do I know? I was just trying to quiet him down and he fell on the floor. Next thing I know they was saying he's dead."

"Who said so?"

"Some woman came in and put her hand on his neck and said so. That's all I know."

Alphie, getting a bit shaky asked, "Well, why are you here?"

"Cause I had to use my nightstick to get him quiet! They say he may have died cause of a bump on his head. He was a mean looking nigger and strong. I had to do something. Did you bring my gun?"

"Yeah, what are you going to do?"

"I'm gonna get out of here, that's what I'm gonna do."

"The car's parked beside the building with the keys in it." She reached down into her handbag and gave him the gun from under her coat.

"Is it loaded?"

"I guess so. That's your business."

Newt took the gun, quickly looked at the chamber to see and opened the door. "I need to use the toilet; I'll be right back."

With that said, he headed out and towards the front door. It was standing open but the screen door was shut. He burst through the door with the detective and the chief close behind.

Unloading the patrol car beside the station house was the rookie cop, Jerry Lester. He had a Tommy gun in his hands when he heard the Chief shouting, "Shoot him! He's armed and dangerous. Shoot the sonuvagun."

Jerry was momentarily frozen and then raised the machine gun to hip level and pulled the trigger. The blast found its target and the prisoner fell to the ground.

In the meantime, the desk sergeant closed the door to the interrogation room with Alphie inside.

"Chief, is he dead? I didn't know what to do. I was just cleaning out your car and all I had was this big gun. I hope I didn't kill him."

"I hope not, too."

Two deaths in one day would be record for Fort Anthony.

At that time of the night, the city was shut up tight as a drum except for some country club types who were on their way home from a Friday night dance and bingo session. The college president Fred Trotman and his wife Eleanor were cruising around town to check on students who might be up to no good. Upon hearing the shots, they drove toward the sound and came upon the scene.

"What happened, Chief?" Fred asked.

"An ex–student from your place was up to no good and got himself shot."

"Is he dead?"

"I think so. We're waiting for the coroner to declare one way or the other."

"Who is the coroner in Fort Anthony?"

"Mr. Oakes."

"The funeral director?"

"Yes sir."

"Is he an MD?"

"No, sir."

Miss Alphie Saine broke out of the front screen door shouting. "Have you shot and killed my Newt? He wasn't going to hurt nobody. He just lost his head and run out that door trying to get away from you cops. He told me you had him framed for killing that nigger man and he said he was innocent!"

She fell on his body and sobbed, "He was a good man. He worked hard to do the right thing and always treated me good. He was a church going man who was well respected out there."

She stood up to attack Chief Mankiwitz. "Dammit, Al, you knew him for twenty years. You know he was innocent. Why did you have to shoot him?"

"Miss Alphie I did not shoot him. Newt was under arrest for assault and was a suspect in a murder investigation. He aimed his revolver at me but the officer shot him as he was turning the corner trying to get away. The officer was following standard procedure and my orders. Newt was armed and dangerous and the officer used the only weapon he had available. Why did you feel it was necessary to bring him that revolver? If he had not been armed he would still be alive?"

Alphie fell back to the ground at Newt's feet and began shouting "Praise God, Hallelujah, take this good man to your bosom, Lord. He was a peacekeeper, not a murderer. Newt Saine loved Jesus. Praise God he is in glory with Jesus. He was murdered and deserves redemption and the love of Christ."

With that, she took his gun out of Newt's hand, put it in her mouth and pulled the trigger. She blew her brains out.

Fred and Eleanor Trotman were aghast. Eleanor fainted and fell into the arms of her husband. He helped her to the car and laid her on the front seat.

"God almighty, Manny, what is going on around this place? Who started this mayhem?"

Ed Negley and the Detective Merlin Stringfellow were helplessly standing outside the screen door watching the tragedy unfold.

"Well, that was a waste of time. Probably saved the state a lot of money though," was the cynical observation of the Detective.

"You are one cold cookie. Who shot him?"

"I think it was the rookie."

"He'll have a few nightmares."

"Yeah, you should go over and see if you can help the couple in the car."

"That's the College President and his wife. Looks like she may have fainted. Shame she had to witness this. I'll go over."

"Doctor Trotman, I will need a statement from you and Mrs. Trotman. In the morning or sometime tomorrow will be fine. You should take her home before something else unexpected happens."

"Thank you, Merlin. I appreciate that."

"Chief, I didn't mean to kill him. I just pulled the trigger and that gun just exploded. What should I do?"

"Finish what you started and go on home. Merlin will want a full statement in the morning."

Elwood Oakes pulled up in a hearse to pick up the corpse and write the coroners report. "Merciful goodness what happened?"

"I'll tell you later. Help us get this mess cleaned up."

Oakes leaned over the body of the man and said, "Whoeee, this guys guts are in a mess. He's dead for sure."

He turned to the woman sprawled across her late husband's feet.

"And her brains are missing. What a mess. You want me to put both of them in the same hearse?"

"Just treat them with respect, Elwood. That's all I ask. Treat em like they were your brother and sister."

"Then have somebody to call the office and have them bring the backup hearse. Who is going to pay for this brother and sister?"

"Till you hear different from me, know that the city will pay the bill."

Chapter Seventy-Five

At the residence of Randy and Rose Roberts
Saturday Morning, May 18, 1935

"Mary Ella, does Elder Ricketts have kin people here in town?"

"None that I heard about. I just know that he has a sister in Indianapolis. He was on his way to see her last night."

"Who would know how to reach her, her name and where she lives?"

"I 'spect that Bishop Stone could help."

"Can he be reached by phone?"

"I'll try. Miss Roberta has anybody told him about Elder Ricketts?"

"I suppose we will find out soon enough. Be prepared for anything. We need to talk about a funeral but that can wait. Just tell him what you know and ask him about the sister."

"Yes'm."

Roberta had stayed with Mary Ella overnight. They were both crushed by the killing of their friend and could give one another moral support. Mary Ella was afraid to stay alone, and Roberta welcomed the opportunity for female company.

Roberta saw Ed Negley coming up the steps. She greeted him at the door with a fond embrace and he kissed her. She kissed him back. She fixed him a cup of coffee and some buttered toast. They sat at the kitchen table, and he began the horror story that unfolded last night.

Roberta, in tears, said, "Poor Eleanor. I need to call her. This is awful, just because I gave Mr. Ricketts a nice 50-dollar bonus and suggested that he might want to go to Chicago."

Calming Roberta, Ed said, "For gosh sakes don't begin blaming yourself. Merlin Stringfellow said the man who killed Ricketts was a former politician who belonged to the Klan. His luck had run out when his boss, some judge, was sent to prison. His name was Newt Saine and his wife was Alphie Scott Saine. Merlin told me he thought she was Klan as well."

Roberta asked, "Did he still have all the money?"

Frustrated, Ed said, "By the time I got to see his body, the money was gone. Fifty dollars is a lot of money and a big temptation to the thug that ran or even a funeral home attendant."

Roberta asked, "Why do you think it was one of them?"

Ed answered, "I'm pretty sure the money was in his pocket at the bus station where they picked up the body."

"Alphie came by the bank to get her money out and really gave me a hard time. Come to think of it all the women who came to the bank yesterday were connected to the Klan. They call themselves 'Women of the Klan.' Most of them go to the same church and they are all Republicans. They give every thing they touch a bad name."

"What church?" asked Ed

"The Old Mellenialite Church. Very fundamental but the preacher is very nice."

"What's his name? Ferdinand Philpot, around town they call him Reverend Ferdy the Birdie. Not much respect for a preacher."

Ed laughed, "I'm not surprised. With a name like that I'm surprised they don't call him worse."

"I guess the Police Chief knows all this."

Ed agreed, "Probably. We need to call Randy."

Chapter Seventy-Six

Spreading the Bad News
May 18, 1935

"Randy, how are you and your girlfriend doing. You are not mistreating her are you?"

"I've got a little news for you."

"No, I'll be around for a while yet. Mr. Ed Ricketts is dead."

"Randy, he was killed over at the bus station last night by some goon or the bus station security officer."

"Yeah, you knew him."

"Right, past tense, it means he is no longer with us. He has gone to his reward or punishment as the case may be. They were questioning him at the police station. Alphie came by the station, they let her see him and she gave him his piece. He ran and a rookie cop mowed him down with a Tommy gun. He tried to escape and they killed him. Blew his guts out. Then the dangdest thing happened. Alphie came out to his body, kneeled down beside him, picked up his piece and blew her brains out. President Trotter and his wife saw it. She fainted and he took her home. I hated to call you, but you had to know. I'm sorry."

"Yeah, Randy and you need to stay stuck for a couple of more days. Roberta and I have things under control here. You know she is pretty terrific."

"Don't worry. That's the story from here. Roberta is staying over here with Mary Ella because she is frightened and they can support each other. She will know where to reach me over the weekend." 'Will do, bossman. We're doing fine here considering the situation we got. I'll let you know when the driver will be there."

Randy gave Rose the entire story. She was in tears soon but he cheered her up when he told her Roberta and Ed Negley had struck up a friendship that was more that just business."

Rose laughed, "Funny business, I'll bet!"

"Maybe."

Chapter Seventy-Seven

Monday May 20, 1935
The Temple Residence

Little Easy Temple was the only soul in Fort Anthony and the surrounding communities unaware of the events taking place around him. Life continued as it was without a care in the world. His grand-mama was cool and calm around him. His daddy was careful to keep him out of sight and in fact, the entire family had been laying low for several weeks.

The school year had ended and Ez was ready for a few days break in his schedule.

Ez knew he would need to get ready for the wake and funeral for Elder Ricketts.

The house issue had not been settled and Esther was able to make the little shack on newly named "Pleasant Hill Road" clean and comfortable. She told Ez to forget about a house in town. That with all the improvements going on around them she would prefer to live in the "Pleasant Hill" neighborhood. After all, they would soon have a park, city water, a new street with sidewalks and all the amenities not available to many communities. She and Ez would fix up this place. It would be better and cause a lot less trouble for everyone. Uncle Hannibal would be thrilled to have her near. She heard the talk around town and knew the danger of stirring up more trouble for their many friends.

Ez agreed that since he was scheduled to start graduate school soon at Indiana University she would be happier surrounded by her church friends. He felt certain that she would find a place of leadership at the church and in the neighborhood since her politics were unknown and strong leadership was needed.

President Trotman assured Ez and Esther that they were welcome on the campus and he looked forward to having them as faculty members next school year. He would follow their lead as to what they were most comfortable doing. He also assured them that the maintenance crew would find time to make minor repairs as needed.

The New Awakenings Baptist Church had already met several times in the auditorium at Western Indiana State Teachers College. The invitation by President Trotman had been generous but the result was un-foreseeable.

Since the group began meeting there on April 28, the Sunday after Easter, the attendance for every service was more than the last. It seems that some of the members of the college choir were interested in joining the group. Associate Professor Ezra Temple heard about that in the hospital and could not wait to get back to check out the situation. Some colored children from Pleasant Hill came to see what the school looked like and some to try out for the choir. Their parents came with them and on Sunday mornings as well. The classrooms near the auditorium were used by the Christian Education committeee on Sunday morning and where the youth group met on Sunday afternoon. The opportunity to worship in such a "spacious and well-equipped place" was a fine opportunity for the little Baptist Church.

It was late spring and the weather remained very moderate. Every one knew that the summer would be hot and dry as would the auditorium. But the opportunity was better than any other option they could imagine!

The funeral for Elder Ricketts would not be held soon. The kin-people of the good man must be notified and arrangements must be made that were satisfactory to them.

Chapter Seventy-Eight

It Was a Fine Funeral
Monday Afternoon, May 20, 1935

A minor controversy arose about the funeral and burial costs for Alpharetta and Newt Saine. Brother Ferdinand Philpot was the pastor at the Old Millienialite Church that was attended by these other unfortunate participants in what became known as "The Bus Station Murder."

Brother Philpot was also a part time funeral director and an earnest competitor with the Oakes Funeral Home. The police chief had sent the bodies to the Oakes establishment with the assurance that the city would pay necessary expenses. Chief Mankiwitz settled after a phone call to Ed Negley who committed the bank to a $250.00 cash contribution to the Old Millienialite Church to cover all expenses and sent a pall for each casket.

But there was still talk: Were the Mayor, the County Judge and other dignitaries who came to all wakes, baptisms and funerals looking for votes? Their absence was noted at the visitation/wake on Monday night.

By Tuesday morning, the problem was cured. Every hack politician in the county appeared for the funeral and to sign the book. Floral arrangements were plentiful and the crowd ample to satisfy even the most ornery Kluxer or other enemy of the city and county leadership. They didn't like them, but they longed for their votes!

Pastor Ferdy took advantage of the full house. He preached a tearjerker and sang every "blood" hymn in the book. Six friends gave testimonies to the goodness of the deceased. The pastor made three altar calls after the service and one at the cemetery. The deacons took up a collection and carried the caskets up the hill to the open graves. The Elders were the honorary pallbearers and four of them offered long prayers for the deceased. The men were dressed in suits and ties or fresh pressed overalls and blue shirts and the ladies were in white summer dresses. Babies cried and older children became testy and were removed to a shade tree in the side yard where they were overseen by three teenage girls.

It was a great day for Brother Philpot and his flock of premillienialist believers. He thought to himself that we should do this more often!

Chapter Seventy-Nine

Back Home in Indiana
Tuesday Evening, May 21, 1935

Ed sent a car and driver for Randy and Rose. They returned to Fort Anthony late Tuesday evening.

Mary Ella was demonstrably glad to see them. Hugs, kisses and "welcome homes" were plentiful. Ed and Roberta were there waiting to hear all about their vacation. Not to be!

Randy and Rose wanted to hear all about the goings on that had even made the Chicago paper.

Since nothing else would do and Mr. Roberts was the boss, the three unburdened their hearts and spilled it all in his lap.

Instead, Randy was not prepared for so much, so after about an hour and a half, he called a halt to the unfolding story until he could absorb what he had heard so far. The next two hours were spent answering dozens of questions from Rose and Randy.

Wisely, Ed Negley had prepared a complete write-up on the activities of the last week. Roberta had proofed it and Mary Ella had added a few touches. The report was 56 double-spaced pages.The internal binder was labeled

PERSONAL AND CONFIDENTIAL
RANDOLPH ROBERTS'
EYES ONLY
May 21, 1935

"This looks pretty official, Ed. Can Rose read it?"

"Give her some time to get back home and into her routine."

"Am I a member of this team or not, Ed?" Rose was miffed.

"Rose, I was hired to give expert advice, and my recommendation to Randy in this instance was part of it. I truly hope the two of you will respect my wisdom."

"We understand," Randy said.

"I think it's time we said good-night. We look forward to more time tomorrow. By the way, Randy and Rose there is something that both of you need to know and I will ask Roberta to tell you."

A wide grin spread across Mary Ella's face.

"Ed and I are going to marry."

"When?" was the first word from Rose.

"Soon," they both answered in unison.

Randy jumped up to hug them both and said, "I knew it. I just knew something good would come out of all this!"

Mary Ella said, "This has been the most exciting week of my life. I was watching them. They are sure enough in love. Roberta asked me to stand up with her."

"Randy would you stand up with me?"

"Ed, don't you take her away from here. I'll fire both of you if you do!"

"We are thinking about a honeymoon in Lake Geneva."

"That will be our wedding gift to you. You will love the honeymoon suite."

With tongue in cheek, Randy grinned and said, "I recommend a day or two in Chicago to visit the wonderful new museums there."

"Randy, I am from Chicago. But that's a good idea!"

"You two lovebirds come by for breakfast in the morning and we can make plans." Rose now had a project to get her mind off other less important things.

Chapter Eighty

Rest for the Weary
Late May 21, 1935

Ed took Roberta to her place above Abe Shunarah's store and went to his room at the hotel. There was a lot yet to do and he sat down to make a list. It wasn't long before he dozed off. He and Roberta had been carrying a large load for the last few days and they were both exhausted. They needed a good nights rest in their own beds!

The morning came quickly. He forced himself out of bed at first light to shower and dress for the day. He glanced through the curtains to see it was raining. "Farmers need the rain this time of year" he thought, "this is Indiana where the economy depends on the right weather at the right time and this was the right time for rain." He felt good. He was ready for whatever lay ahead. It lifted his spirits. The rain gave him hope that whatever problems he came to discover and help solve could soon be cleaned up and he could get on with his life. His had been a life of drought and storms, of good and poor harvests, of a plethora or a dearth of the good things in life. He was on a new adventure with a new partner.

His only other venture in which two became one was a total failure. He joined the army and was sent to France as a historian. He was to record the battles and skirmishes, the vicissitudes of life in the army, and after the Armistice to follow the Versailles Conference and write the story there too. He married in a fever just before he went overseas. He was furloughed after the Armistice and went home to be with his young bride. He caught the train to Detroit from New York and took a cab out to Grosse Point to her parents' home. Things went downhill from there. Her parents were shocked to see him and she was not at home. She had gone to California to pursue a dream or so it said in the Dear John letter presented to him by her parents. They were heart-broken for Ed since they liked him very much. Two plus years away was no fun for her and she was all about fun.

With no more questions, Ed went to his priest and asked if he could get the marriage annulled. Father Phillip was sympathetic but did not offer much hope. Father Phillip attempted reconciliation with Lillian but to no avail. She was living with another man and was not about to give up this lifestyle she liked so much for some Second Lieutenant Army history writer. Ed's brother was an attorney and offered to settle the matter. Ed simply said, "Whatever I need to sign, send it to me." He went back to France and spent four years there covering Europe for the Army Times and stringing for the Tribune on the side. When he came home in 1921, he had a job in Chicago waiting for him. Life as a confirmed bachelor could be dark and drear at times but mostly free of heartbreak.

He honked the horn happily for Roberta and she was ready for the day as well. They liked early mornings. "I get so much more done when I don't sleep late" was her mantra.

Prior to going over to see Randy and Rose they stopped in the Java Club for a cup of black coffee for him and tea for her. They were falling into a routine already. A routine they liked and that helped them realize how much they had missed when alone.

Mary Ella greeted them at the door with a twinkle in her eye.

Roberta had become good friends with this lovely, refined person. They had often speculated about their futures as single women in a broken world. They both agreed that they were very lucky to have landed employment with this family. Roberta had attended business school in Indianapolis as a young person many years before. Mary Ella graduated from high school with high honors in Dayton, Ohio and earned a scholarship to Earlham College. Both her parents were college graduates as were all of her siblings. Good jobs were hard to find and she responded to an inquiry at the office of the Dean of Women. The Dean told her that working for a wealthy young couple in a nice, quiet, small mid-west town was not a bad thing these days.

Chapter Eighty-One

Wedding Bells
Early Morning of May 22, 1935

Randy and Rose greeted them at the door with a hug and smiles all around. They were surprised at their sudden announcement but they were mature adults who desired to make the most of the next twenty or thirty years! They were like two twenty year olds. As Mary Ella put it, "They were eat up with love." What else was there to do?

The light breakfast of pastry, juice and hot coffee for the men and tea for the ladies went nicely.

The events of the preceding weeks were reported in detail, and the preliminary report prepared by Ed, Roberta, and Sam was dissected in some detail.

Plans for the Ricketts funeral and burial were not nearly complete. Nevertheless, a discussion was held about what his kin-people would want to do. It was really in their hands, so waiting was their only option. No sense in meddling where you may not be wanted.

The plan envisioned by Ed and augmented by Roberta was not revolutionary but it was thorough.

STUDY OF THE BANKING MARKET IN AND AROUND
FORT ANTHONY, INDIANA
Confidential Report for
Randolph Williams Roberts,

Chairman and President of the Bank of Fort Anthony, Indiana

"IF YOU KEEP ON DOING WHAT YOU HAVE BEEN DOING THEN YOU WILL KEEP ON GETTING WHAT YOU HAVE BEEN GETTING!"

Brief sections revealing the findings from 20 major customers of the bank, 20 depositors and 20 small loan recipients followed the introduction.

The summary featured responses to the positive as well as the negative findings. The positive responses had to do with the helpful spirit around loans and collections. Randy got high marks for his community spirit and leadership. The connection of the bank with the HOLC and other federal government programs also received high marks.

The negative report was more comprehensive since this is what the bank board and leadership needed to know:

- Mr. Roberts spends too much city money on poor folks
- Mr. Roberts entertains too much
- Colored people get more favorable treatment than do others
- Sam the Cashier is disagreeable
- The interior of the bank is too dark
- Mr. Roberts is too much a politician and does not pay enough attention to his customers
- Interest on loans is too high
- Interest paid on savings deposits is too low
- The city accounts should be in an account in Indianapolis
- Property taxes are too high
- Mr. Roberts gives too much money to the Methodist Church
- The Methodists get favorable treatment
- The bank is too hot in the summer and too cold in the winter

Et cetera, et cetera.

"That's the biggest pile of crap I ever saw!" was Randy's immediate response.

Ed responded, "It's not scientific but it's what I heard, overheard and heard again."

"Hell, Ed, I could have told you that while you were still in Chicago!"

Rose chimed in, "Maybe we should shut the bank down and get the hell out of here!"

Ed asked, "What would Father Beckham say to that, Rose?"

And next, "What will he say to this, Randy?"

"Nothing if he never sees it! It is addressed to me and is confidential and I plan to keep it that way!"

Ed and Roberta were quiet. Ed knew it was a bad idea to share this with Rose, but Roberta persuaded him that she needed to know. Randy has so much on his mind that a sympathetic wife is what he needs. Roberta calculated Rose might respond as she did but would soon come around. She did not get off the last bus and knew better than to pop off like this. "Maybe this is good" Roberta hoped to herself.

Roberta spoke first, "Tell you what Ed; you and Randy go on over to the bank and glad hand the staff and the customers. Rosie and I will stay here and get things in order. She has been away for a while and I will help answer her mail and other things."

Chapter Eighty-Two

To the Bank
Later on the Morning, May 22, 1935

It was a nice morning, so Ed and Randy walked to the bank. Ed felt a bit jaunty, so he removed his linen jacket and tossed it over his left shoulder since he could still shake hands with his right. Randy followed suit, so to speak.

They arrived at the bank a little after nine. Sam had opened up and all was in order for the 8:30 opening time. Ed and Randy looked dapper as they walked up the granite steps to the entry, two brass doors with the bank name and regular hours in gold leaf painted on the heavy plate glass inserts.

Randy went in first. All was exceedingly somber. From the tellers cage on the far end came a quiet tapping on the marble deal plate. "Welcome Home" broke the silence and all joined in with polite applause for Randy. He was a little shocked.

"Hello everyone. I am glad to be home with each of you."

Next came quiet tapping from the other cage. "Congratulations to Ed and Roberta." Ed was shocked. News like theirs gets around quickly in small towns, he thought.

Randy went to each employee and gave him or her a hug except for Sam the Cashier. "Glad to see you Sam. Thanks for all the help and leadership while I was away."

"Of course, that is my job."

"What a cold fish," thought Randy.

"C'mon in Ed. Cup of coffee? Pull up a chair."

"A little cool water will do. I'll get it." He had learned the location of the Dixie Cups and water cooler by now.

They sat at the small mahogany game table Randy used for customer sit-down meetings. The top was inset with pink marble, so it gave a little class to an otherwise dull office.

"Well, let's don't waste any time responding to our customers," Randy said with a grin.

"This is serious stuff Randy and if this bank is to survive in this town you need to get ahead of the curve."

"Okay, so what's first?"

"You tell me, you're the one with the big hairy balls."

"I asked you first." Randy was being a bit childish but Ed caught the gist and proceeded to give his best advice.

"Here's my list in no particular order. What I don't cover is already working:

1. "Take care of your employees. Work out a career ladder.

2. Dress them up a bit. Give the women a clothes allowance and buy them four new outfits a year.

3. Pay attention to their birthdays and their children's birthdays.

4. Give Sam an allowance as well. Buy him a tux for ABA Events and send him to them. Put a boutonniere in his lapel. Encourage him to join the Kiwanis and pay his dues. Smile at him a lot.

5. Install a new heating and air conditioning system. Be the most comfortable place in town.

6. Buy the empty store building next door and use it for community meetings. It's cheap-less than five grand. Heat and cool it like the bank.

7. Paint the interior of the bank to get rid of the gray walls that match the gray marble columns.

8. Improve the lighting all around.

9. Be certain your rates are highly competitive. Pay a little more and charge a little less.

10. Require your city finance officer to put the city deposits out on competitive bid. Include all FDIC insured banks in Indiana and other National Banks.

11. Get a rumor out to the Board of Aldermen, the Methodist Church Woman's Missionary Society and the Pleasant Hill folks that you are considering stepping down as mayor. See what happens.

12. From where I stand the problem here at the bank and in Fort Anthony generally stems from groups of women who parade under different flags but are from the old "Women in the Klan of Indiana."

13. The Klan here in Indiana is top heavy with women. Although almost every elected official in Indiana in the twenties were Kluxers and many were sent to jail for one reason or another, the women were behind each of them. They also were dominant in the Republican Party, the American Legion and some churches. After their men were beat down by the law and the voters, the women took up the cudgels! They berated the men for not sticking to their guns and came out as a very powerful "behind the scenes" force to be reckoned with. You and your bank are paying the price that is being extracted by the Women of the Klan in Indiana!"

The office of the President of the First National Bank of Fort Anthony suddenly became quiet, dank and cold. Randy's eyes became moist. Ed felt badly that he had unloaded all this on him in one morning. Randy was in danger of going back into his former depressed state.

"Let's go over to the club for an early lunch. I think a stiff martini would help me out right now."

Ed knew better,"Let's put a big smile on our face and I will call Vern Shipley and we will drop in on him for a visit. He knows we might drop by."

"Can we go by the club after that?"

"If you want to do that, after we visit with Vern."

Chapter Eighty-Three

Study of Reverend Vernon Shipley
Minister of the First Methodist Church
Early Afternoon, May 22, 1935

Reverend Vern Shipley welcomed them. "Come in friends. I'm glad to see you back, Randy. Here Ed, have a seat. What is on your minds?"

Randy struggled with his words, "I need some help and advice."

"From me or the Lord?"

"I guess I need an intermediary. I seem unable to muster up the courage to do it all myself."

With Ed's help, Randy went over the key points in the discussion and the findings from Ed's survey.

"Sounds like you need a business consultant or maybe a specialist from the ABA."

"How about you give it a go, Reverend." It was Ed in his offhand and relaxing way to get the session started.

"Why don't we begin with a prayer?" Vern moved to the door and quietly closed it.

"Gracious God, we stand before You as three in the wilderness. This good man, your servant Randy is hurting mightily and needs Your healing power. Bless us as we seek to bring him back to wholeness through Your love and grace. In the name of Jesus the Christ through whom all who wish to have it receive Your power."

Randy asked Ed to tell Vern about his findings and recommendations.

After doing so, Ed asked to be excused so Vern and Randy could work through being a confessing Christian and dealing with problems of business, politics, and community.

Vern asked Louise Lund to bring them a snack to tide them over.

The session lasted until almost 4 p.m.

Ed asked Louise to call him when the session was over so that he could pick up Randy. He received the call at 4:15 and picked Randy up at 4:30.

Ed had briefed Rose and Roberta and suggested that they have supper early at a country tea room in an old house outside of town.

Randy was subdued but pleasant. Rose and Roberta were like a couple of clucking hens while Ed and Randy listened to the idle conversation. Both men wished for a drink to soothe their aching minds. Both knew better!

Randy broke the ice. "Ed, tell them the big problem you think we have and what you recommend."

On the way home, Rose opened fire: "That common gossip, worthless heifer Etta Rains will get a piece of my mind when I see her next. Swap and Shop-I'll swap and shop her. Don't we sponsor her on the radio and isn't she a big Bible Study leader at her pissant little church over next to Bill Waller's hog farm?"

"Take it easy Rose. Randy and Ed will take care of her some how. Our job is to remain calm and let them handle the situation."

"I knew this political crap would come to no good and those worthless coloreds over on Hardscuffle should get off their asses and take care of their own dang messes! I'm sick of all of this. Ed you figure out how you and Randy can dump all of this, and we can move somewhere that people will appreciate a good man like Randy who thinks he is still a Boy Scout or an altar boy kissing every foot in this county."

With that, she leaned her head back and began to sob.

Chapter Eighty-Four

Meeting of the Board of Directors
First National Bank of Ft. Anthony
Wednesday, June 5, 1935

"Good Morning."

It was Randy Roberts, Chair of the Board opening the meeting. The board met at least once a quarter.

"Would the Secretary please call the roll?"

With her usual efficiency, Roberta called the roll of the four members. "All members present, Mr. Chairman."

The membership of the board was closely held: Randy, Rose, Father Beckham and Fred Trotman.

"I have the minutes and financial report prepared for your review. Things are in good order as you can easily see. Deposits are up, gross income on loans is up and expenses are as budgeted. May I hear a motion for approval?"

The motion was made by Fred Trotman and seconded by Rose.

"I have been in close communication with each of you during the last quarter and you know that your local executive committee has encouraged me to look for ways to stay ahead of the competition in what will surely be an improving market.

1. I have contracted with Lee Brothers out of Indianapolis to install a complete heating and air conditioning system. We will be the first bank outside of Indianapolis and Chicago to do so.

2. Solomon Bros. & Oden Company out of Louisville will completely redecorate and furnish the interior and clean and paint the exterior. They are the best! As you can see, it needs attention.

3. I have negotiated a favorable purchase contract for the adjacent vacant building and with your approval will proceed to acquire it and remodel it for use as a new boardroom and community meeting hall.

4. We plan a catering kitchen and other suitable amenities for civic clubs and ladies groups to meet. This will attract new customers in our doors. I expect a payback time of no more than four years with a return on our investment of thousands of future depositors.

5. I have initiated an employee benefit plan on top of the new Roosevelt Social Security scheme.

6. We have granted our employees a small allowance for clothing and furnishings. We are proud of them and we can attract the best employees with more benefits like these.

7. They will be happier and very proud to tell their neighbors where they work. They will have use of the kitchen next door in the annex as well as free access for meetings of their organizations.

I have encouraged Sam Huntley, our cashier, to hook up with the Kiwanis Club and encourage them to use our new meeting space. The charge for weekly usage will be minimal. For occasional use by bank customers there will be no charge.

"We will continue to solidify our customer base among old time members of this community. We will work hard for the business of new potential customers. Whoever they may be and wherever they may live and work. We will reach out and we will remain the premier bank in this area!

"I have spoken briefly to the members of the Board of Aldermen and told them I would count on them to bear more of the load of making our city the best small town in Indiana. It is my declared intent to lead the finest bank of this area and the finest small city as well. When my duties with the city become too burdensome I will turn them over to a successor and give my full attention to this bank. Thank you."

Fred Trotman spoke for the first time. "Friends we have an exceptional young man leading this city and this bank. We are the envy of all who know our story. I move to approve the plans laid out so articulately by our Chairman Randy Roberts."

Father Beckham seconded the motion.

It passed unanimously.

"I move we adjourn to the club for lunch," said Father Beckham.

"Father, I have a better idea. Let's all adjourn to the Riverview Tea Room out on the Wabash."

"If it suits you, Rose, it suits me."

Chapter Eighty-Five

Good Housekeeping
Thursday, June 6, 1935

While everything was settled at the Roberts household, the work was just getting underway with Ezra and his family.

More than two weeks had passed since the college graduation and the musical that had been postponed to correspond with the graduation celebration on Friday, the 17th of May. This gave Ez, his students and others extra time to prepare. There was an enthusiastic crowd for their premiere production.

Ez totally healed from his injuries was in top form, as were the choir and musicians. The graduation went well and Ezra was pleased that all but two of his students were returning. This assured him that he had done a good job and he would have a good start on the year with some qualified musicians.

The presence of Esther made life happier by any measure. Esther accomplished some serious cleaning and repairs. Esther put Ezra to work as well. He typically avoided domestic duties and had not changed his way since they moved into the little house on Hardscuffle Road.

When Esther came home with some Wallrite to cover the rough walls and ceilings, she taught him how to hang wallpaper. When the heavy paper felt was up, she declared she wanted to paint a couple of the rooms. He was ready to leave home or send her back where she came from. After a struggle, they completed the job in a manner suitable to Esther and she said jokingly, "You and Easy can take a few days off to play around. By the way that raggedy looking yard is our next project so the two of you might want to play with a rake in your hands."

In the evenings, she continued to tutor Easy to prepare for the first grade soon. His music lessons went by the wayside for a few weeks. She had a strong desire to have him ready for the first grade at the Demonstration School. She knew he could do the work because he was easily persuaded to work hard and apply himself.

After graduation and the musicale, they had immersed themselves in the improvements to the house. Even though it was a rental property, Esther spent her own money to buy the supplies. However, she lived up to her commitment to visit the local churches and continue her steady attendance at The New Awakenings Baptist Church.

Fort Anthony was beginning to change from the typical provincial town, the trademark of the Midwest, to a small city with a more cosmopolitan approach to life and culture. Cities can rise like the phoenix or fall flat as a flitter after the drama of the recent spring and winter.

The tragedy with Elder Ricketts, the death of Lilah and her baby, the fire at the soon to be rebuilt Pleasant Hill Baptist Church were hard to absorb in some parts of town. The change in the approach to customer service by the bank; the upgrades to old Hardscuffle Road; the wedding of Ed and Roberta Noble at City Hall was some of the good news. A program to upgrade Main Street with financing by the local banks and help from the FERA was welcomed by all the citizens of Fort Anthony.

On recommendation of the state planning authority, the city hired a part-time city manager to take charge of the anticipated growth and more complex business activities. Ed Noble applied for and was appointed by the city council with Louise Edwards as his biggest supporter.

Although the interest in a symphony orchestra waned, the townspeople realized the asset represented by the college. Ellie and Fred Trotman began to host more events to reinforce the relationship between the town and the gown. His plans for the next year included: events open to the public, guest speakers, more music and drama, adult classes in the evening and lots of comp tickets to athletic events funded by the bank.

Esther Temple turned out to be an important addition to the city. She was elected chair of the Pleasant Hill Improvement Association, a frequent guest speaker at all sorts of events and the mother of the very popular Ezra Temple.

The leading lights of the city, learning of her outstanding education at Fisk University in Nashville, of her lengthy experience teaching in the primary grades, her personal charm and her experience living on a college campus as the wife of one of the leaders at a state school gave her a boost and open invitations to all the important places and events.

Of course, it could not have hurt to be the guest of people like the Shipley's, the Edwards, the Barclays, and the Roberts. She was neither ambitious nor self aggrandizing, she was a good woman with a lot of class.

"Mrs. Temple, this is Ed Noble at the bank…I am happy you and Ezra have a phone now. We will have lots to talk about. You know the bank has acquired the building next door and turned it into a community room…I would like to come by and pick you up. We can have lunch and come by the bank so you can look at the new facilities; how about tomorrow?…I will come by your house then. Do you enjoy the food at the hotel or the Tea Room?…Fine, see you at 11:30."

For the last several days, Ezra had been in touch with the Dean at IU on the newly acquired telephone. Dean Goodrich said to call collect, so Ez felt it was okay to use the telephone for his out of town business. His plan was to try to start some summer classes soon.

"Ezra, get Easy cleaned up, dinner will be ready in a little while."

"Yessum. Easy get in here boy, Granny has supper almost ready."

"Can I come back out after supper?"

"Sure, we can play a little catch."

"Henry wants to play kick-the-can with Sylvia and Will."

"That will be fine, too. Come on in now."

"Okay" he said mournfully.

Chapter Eighty-Six

After Dinner
Thursday, June 6, 1935

"Easy, you stick close to the house."

Esther was concerned. "Ezra, Mr. Noble at the bank called me to invite me to lunch. We are going to the Tea Room tomorrow. Will that cause him any problems?"

"I don't think so. Why do you ask?"

"Well, you know how things around have been especially at the bank."

"Shouldn't be a problem for you. He is a big boy and I am sure that the Mayor is behind his invitation."

"What should I wear?" Esther asked.

"Nothing very fancy. Do you know if Lilah's things fit you?"

"I never thought about it. Would you care?"

"Course not. I bet she would be proud to see you in some of her outfits."

He went to Lilah's closet and selected a lovely cotton dress she had not worn but once.

"Try this on."

Although Esther was 25 years older than Lilah, she had a similar figure and was firm from years in the classroom working with children. She was surprised when she slipped on the dress and it fit her.

"Look at me," she beckoned to Ezra.

"That's almost perfect. It is a little loose around the middle. I think Lilah bought that when she was beginning to show with the baby."

"I can fix that pretty quick," she said with a pleased grin.

When Easy came in from his game he found his grandmother sewing on a dress and had laid a hat and gloves on her bed.

"You going somewhere, Granny?"

"I am having lunch with my banker tomorrow."

Ezra came in, "Easy leave your granny alone she's busy. Let's go back to your room and read some."

It was a surprise to Ez that Easy wanted to read to him. "Where did you learn to read so well?"

"Granny taught me."

"She is a good granny isn't she?"

"And a good cook too," he said as he rubbed his tummy.

"Easy, you know that I will be on the road a lot this summer and next year. You will be the man around the house and I want you to help Granny. Will you do that?"

"Does Granny know that?"

"We have talked about it. I need to go back to school and get more education so I can be a better teacher. I will be here some every week and we can play catch, and read and walk up to the top of the hill with a picnic lunch."

"You can stay here and Granny can teach you!"

"I'm certain she could. She has taught me a lot just like she taught you to read and play your music."

"How long will it be?

"I hope no more than a couple of years."

"Maybe I'll be in the second grade by then."

"I hope so. Will you read some to me?"

"I want you to read to me tonight."

"Tell you what. Go clean up a little; put on your pajamas and come back here and I will do just that."

"Mother, I told Easy of my plans. He decided he wanted me to read to him. He usually wants to read to me."

"I'm glad you told him. He needs a little extra attention for the next few days."

Chapter Eighty-Seven

Lunch at the Tea Room
Friday, June 7, 1935

"Easy, I'm going out to lunch. Your father is going to take you down to the creek to find some crawdads or a pretty rock or two. I'll be back in an hour or so."

"I did not plan to do that. I have stuff to finish up at the library. I was going to take him with me over there," Ezra said in a whisper.

"My plan is better," she said with authority and finality.

"Hey, Easy get on your old britches. Leave your shoes at home. We are going wading in the Jones Creek."

At 11:30, Ed Noble knocked on the door. Esther appeared at the screen door, dressed for a tearoom luncheon date in a wide brimmed spring hat with the cotton dress from Lilah's closet with white gloves.

Ed escorted her to his auto and made small talk on the way to the restaurant.

Upon arrival at the Tea Room, Ed parked the car on the street and a hostess led them to a table in the middle of the dining room.

"Does this suit you, Mrs. Temple?" Ed asked.

"Perfectly."

The hostess handed each one a menu and they looked it over.

"A very nice menu. I think I would like the fruit salad and a glass of iced tea," she volunteered.

"That didn't take long," said Ed.

"It will be refreshing and fruit is so good for you. Do you eat here often?"

"I find this is a good place to bring important customers of the bank."

"I'm flattered but we both know I am not important to your bank."

"I hope you will begin to think of us as your bank, Miss Esther! We would like to have your account and your support within the community."

"I don't have hardly any money. I'm new around here."

"You were recently elected to lead your community association and I'll bet you have a few dollars that should be in an interest bearing savings account. I brought the papers to sign you up today. Our president Randy Roberts has assigned me the opportunity to meet all your members and invite them to use our new community room for their meetings. He says he will keep a supply of Dr. Pepper on hand and a pot of coffee for you when you meet there!"

The waitress came and wrote down their orders and excused herself quietly.

"Well, that is nice of him. We will gladly accept his offer and when we get a treasurer I will suggest she deposit the dues money in your bank."

"You are an important customer of our bank already. Can you arrange a meeting of your group soon?"

"I don't see why not. Can I call to set it up?"

"Give me a call anytime and I will arrange it. Here is my card."

The waitress brought their food and disappeared.

Ed had ordered a tomato stuffed with tuna salad and a glass of tea.

"How's your fruit salad."

"Delightful. And your choice?"

"It's not a home-grown tomato but the tuna salad is fine."

After a short time eating and some small talk, Esther asked to be excused. She quickly headed for the ladies room. As she opened the door she vomited and went inside to empty her system of the fruit she had eaten.

Their waitress made no attempt to help her but said to the hostess, "You can take the nigger out of the country but you can't take the country out of the nigger." She grinned broadly at her humor.

The hostess said, "My goodness Lou what an awful thing to say about her. You know who they are?"

"Hell yes, I know who they are and I don't care!"

"Well you just go get a mop and bucket and help me clean up that mess."

Ed hurried to the restroom door and asked Esther if she was okay.

"I'll be out in a minute."

As the waitress and the hostess were cleaning up her vomit, she appeared, "I don't know what came over me, Mr. Noble. Can you take me home now please?"

Ed laid two dollars on the counter and helped her get into the car.

"Are you better now?"

"I think so. I am so embarrassed."

"What happened?"

"To tell you the truth I think some of the fruit was bad. I was barely able to get it down but I did not want to embarrass you, so I ate it. I wish I had not done so!"

"I will get you home and come right back. I want to see what made you sick."

Ed had suddenly realized that taking a colored lady into the "Tea Room" might have been a mistake.

He told himself, "There remained some bad people in Fort Anthony and I think we just ran into one of them."

He took Esther into the house, and she sat down in an overstuffed chair.

"Will you be alright?" he asked. "I need to get back there as soon as possible."

Chapter Eighty-Eight

The Kitchen of the Tea Room
Friday, June 7, 1935

Ed spoke curtly to the hostess, "I want to see the fruit plate or the scrapings of it. Are you accustomed to serving your customers rotten fruit?" He was hot!

She took him to the kitchen and found their plates on a counter.

"Where is our waitress?"

"She said she was sick and left after she cleaned the floor."

"What is her name and where does she live?"

"Wait and I will write it down."

"Madame, I will have you know my guest is new to our city and I brought her to lunch here on business. I won't be doing that with other potential customers."

"Sir, I assure you that will not ever happen again. Actually, I fired Lou and told her she had better get out of town. She would never get another job in this town and in a nice place like this again!"

"Is it possible she served her bad fruit on purpose?"

"Yes, I think that's possible." Then, she repeated what Lou had said about Mrs. Temple.

"I shall try to find her and lock her up if I can!"

"I don't think that is a good idea. Both her parents still hold onto their old Klan connections. He was a court officer ten years ago and she was active in the Legion Auxiliary. He went to jail for some time.

They will cause the bank and the Mayor and the coloreds over on Nigger Hill a lot of problems."

"Will you wrap these two plates in some wax paper? I plan to send them to a lab and have them tested. By the way, the community you referred to is now officially named Pleasant Hill. Please remember that in the future."

Chapter Eighty-Nine

On Pleasant Hill
Mid Afternoon Friday, June 7, 1935

Ezra and Easy returned from Jones Creek shortly after Esther came home.

"Granny, I caught a big crawfish from under a rock. He is in this can. Daddy and I had a great time down at the creek."

He was high as a kite. Ezra joined in: "We really did have fun. We need to do that again. I have a lot to catch up with Easy. He wants to go fishing at the pond over behind the Gulf Station."

"I don't think that would be a good idea. We are not on good terms with the management there. How did he know about it anyway?"

"One of the children on the road told him. I will take him somewhere soon. Are you feeling okay? You look weak in the eyes."

"I ate something that disagreed with me. I'll be okay soon."

Easy crawled up in her lap and said "Oh, grandmama you smell funny."

"You are probably right. I need to freshen up."

Ed Noble strode into the side door of the hospital lab. He carried the bag with the two plates inside the lab and asked for the lab director. He briefly described the incident and told him he would pay for the work that was needed to check out the food for poison or bad bacteria. He was told to come back the next morning. He left his card and requested to be called when the results were known.

He went back to the bank and told Roberta of the events at the tearoom.

"I agree with the hostess. Do not make too much of it. The Tea Room has never served coloreds before you went in with Esther."

Ed was shocked. "I never gave it a thought. I guess I have a lot to learn about my new hometown. What's your advice?"

"Let it lie. Get the lab report and file it away. If Esther has further complications get her to the hospital. Otherwise, drop it."

"How will we become a compassionate and progressive city unless somebody puts their foot down?"

"Ed, a long ditch is dug one shovel full at a time. Don't endanger the work we have done at the bank and the good things happening within our city government."

He was taken aback by the response of his new bride, but Ed knew she was right. "I'll let you know what the hospital comes up with. How about some flowers?"

"Let's take some to her this evening."

The visit to Esther was a positive experience. While Roberta chatted with Esther, Ed told Ez what happened.

Ez said, "Don't worry she will be fine. She did not expect that sort of treatment here but she is a forgiving person and understands the weaknesses of human nature. I am okay, too. Easy and I had a big time at the creek. He caught a crawdad and that is a big deal."

As they drove back to town Roberta could tell that Ed was still upset. "Let's go by the club for a drink and a little something to eat."

Chapter Ninety

Bloomington, Indiana
Sunday Morning, June 10, 1935

It was important for Ez to show up in Bloomington on the eleventh so he had left town on Saturday heading that way. He asked Esther if he could borrow the Peerless and leave his old panel truck with her for a couple of days.

"I am reluctant to do that," she said. "Drive the panel carefully and come back safely."

Ez was disappointed but understood. She had important business to take care of and it would be important for her to have the big car. He had picked up a used tire for a spare and checked the oil when he got some gas at the Gulf station.

The trip was uneventful although it took longer than he thought. It was after dark when he pulled onto the campus. He had decided to sleep in the truck. He pulled up next to the gym so he might find a place to clean up for church the next day. He scavenged an old mattress from the girls' dorm junk heap. The beds were being changed out before the summer session started.

The next morning he made breakfast on some provisions sent by Esther. His jug of water was running low but he could replenish that when he went to shower. He had enough fruit, bread and jam for a couple of days. He would not starve. As he left to shower, he carefully covered all his belongings with the old quilt he used. He locked the doors and went to the gym. It was locked securely. He walked over to a men's dorm, found no one at home but a shower room was open and he enjoyed a cool one.

Walking back to the truck, he noticed a rear door standing open. He ran to see what was up and found an old man going through his belongings.

"Whatcha doing in my truck old man? Come outta there. You are messing up my stuff. You need something? Get out!"

The old man hung his head and said, "I'm hungry. Do you have anything I can eat?"

"You mean you broke into my truck to find some food? I think you were looking for more than food. Here is an apple. Now get outta here!"

The old fellow shuffled off towards the cafeteria.

He rigged a way to secure the two back doors and walked towards a neighborhood where the town folks lived. Although his clothes were rumpled, he was dressed and found a Baptist church nearby. It was still early and he went in to check it out. He was drawn to the chancel where he saw a large pipe organ and a piano. He knew better than to mess with someone's pipe organ, but what could it hurt to try out the baby grand piano? It was a very old Steinway, but it was in tune. He looked under the cover and found it had been recently renovated. There was a brass plate identifying it as property of the University. He thought to himself, "Perhaps the university would sell me one of these for our church when we rebuild."

There was an old hymnal on the piano just waiting to facilitate a brief concert by the maestro.

It was not long until the organist came in. She walked up to the front and asked chidingly, "Who is that sitting in Mama Bear's chair?"

Ez jumped up and began to apologize. "Hey man," she said, "You were hitting some hot licks on Marching to Zion."

"Ma'am," he blurted out, "I was tempted beyond my ability to withstand the opportunity to play such a fine old instrument."

"You are right about one thing. It is old. It was the first one they purchased. They gave it to the church and the church paid a hundred dollars to get it renovated. Plays good, doesn't it?"

"Our church burned down and we will need one when we rebuild. I hope I can be so lucky. Keep your eyes open. I will be around here for a couple of years part-time working on my Master's degree. My name is Ezra Temple. "

"Ezra, I am Celina Goodrich. My husband is the associate dean at the school."

"I'm glad to meet you. I met him when I came up to apply."

"You want to play some today. I think you will know most of our material. Our choir is due now to rehearse. Our service is not until noon. We give our folks time to rest on Sunday morning."

"When do I start?"

"Let me get the organ warmed up and we can begin anytime."

Once again, the crowd of mostly ladies loved Ez. He and Celina had some fun. Dr. Sam Goodrich joined them after the service and praised them both. They invited Ezra to lunch and he readily accepted. They walked over to the school cafeteria and although it did not officially open to students until Monday, the faculty dining room was available. He was hungry. Dean Goodrich asked him when his last meal was.

With a full stomach and some luck, it was another good day for Ezra Temple.

Chapter Ninety-One

Office of Ed Noble
Monday, June 11, 1935

"Mr. Noble, please."

"Mr. Noble, this is Esther Temple. I called to thank you for the flowers."

"I also called to ask a favor. I have talked to some of my neighbors and we would like to accept your offer to hold a meeting at the new Community Room next to the bank."

"Yes I think next week would be just fine."

"Let me tell you what we would like to do. We would like to have a meeting of our neighbors and then have a reception honoring the Mayor and the County Judge. We'll bring the food. Could you help us with the coffee and cold drinks?"

Ed went to Roberta's desk to tell her.

"She called you? That's great. Did you set a date?"

"As soon as possible" he replied.

"Mrs. Temple, this is Ed Noble. How about Tuesday the eighteenth? Both the County Executive and Madame Vice Mayor say that will work for them. Absolutely he will be there. We just wanted to be sure that she would be available. I will come by, pick up your list and see whom we should invite. Good, I'll be by shortly."

"Roberta, the date is set with her."

Roberta asked, "Should we get some invites in the mail or call the list?"

"I think a call will do in this situation."

Chapter Ninety-Two

The Temple Residence
Tuesday, June 12, 1935

It was one week until the neighbors from Pleasant Hill met with the politicians at the bank's new meeting hall. Esther had already sent word up and down the road of the upcoming event. She asked some of them to come by her house this evening to talk about the issues to discuss. While at the meeting she had told Easy he could visit his friend next door to play but stay in the two yards. The meeting was set to begin when Esther heard Easy scream. Suddenly there was a great commotion next door.

She ran out the back door, followed by her committee, to find Easy hanging by his right arm from the wringer of the washing machine on the back porch of her neighbor's house. His friend was standing close by crying, "I didn't do nothing, Miss Esther. He never seen one and wanted to see it work."

Esther immediately hit the lever on top of the wringer to open the rollers and free Little Easy. The rollers had pulled his little arm all the way through and was grinding up the skin and muscle at his armpit. He was bleeding badly and a neighbor brought some towels. It was a confusing and tragic scene. Esther prayed, "O praise God, save this child, look over him and comfort him." The sheriff's office had been called and said they would warn the town hospital that he was on the way. Esther was soaked with blood but managed to stop some of the bleeding by wrapping a towel tightly around the exposed muscles and bone of the little brown arm. All around her they were moaning and crying but Esther kept her senses. When the sheriff appeared in his '33 Ford patrol car she carried the child to the car and held him in her lap on the hurried trip to the hospital.

By the time they reached the Emergency Room he had passed out and was limp as if the angel of death had taken him. Esther was quietly praying all the while, so when the physician took him, she collapsed on the floor. She was assisted to a place to rest while the hospital staff began their triage on Easy.

Few of the staff had seen a more difficult injury to treat! One surgeon who had served in a battlefield hospital in the War appeared as if sent by the Hand from Heaven. He explained that he had heard of the situation at dinner with physician friends in the hospital cafeteria. With no record of the child or the doctor, the staff immediately looked up to the senior physician as he gave orders and laid hands on the child as if he did this sort of thing everyday.

Meanwhile, Ed and Roberta had received word about the tragedy and came immediately. Ed went in to see Esther and agreed to handle the crowd of townspeople who knew of these new neighbors in town and came to pray, to inquire, to offer to help and most of all to offer condolences because almost everyone was certain the child would not survive.

Ed Noble appeared to bring them up to the minute information. "Easy Temple is still alive and breathing. He has been injured badly but he is in good hands, it seems that we have a visitor in our area who is one of the finest surgeons in America. He is here visiting some friends.

"Please continue to pray for Easy and the nurses and doctors who are doing their best to save his life. Mrs. Temple told me to say how grateful she is for your friendship and support and asks for your prayers as well. I feel certain this will be a long surgery so it would be good for us all to leave the rest to the Great Physician and His doctors. Thanks for coming."

Dr. Albert Droulliard is President of the Medical Association that promotes the collective interests of physicians and patients of color. A renowned speaker, he is one of the most sought after men in the Midwest. He is a highly skilled surgeon, is currently the Chief of Staff of the largest, most prestigious hospital in Chicago and an avid sportsman. His hobby is tying dry flies, which gives the fine hand of this surgeon a great advantage.

Roberta and Ed knocked on the door, which had been set up for Esther. They entered and Roberta was shocked at the blood on Esther's dress and arms. It was nearly dry so Roberta insisted that Ed leave the room while Esther cleaned up. He went to their place and picked up a nightgown and robe for Esther. Roberta had arranged for her to remain overnight after the trauma of the evening and Esther agreed to accept the offer.

When Ed returned he inquired of the situation with Easy. A duty nurse said that they were hopeful. The surgeon was the best she had ever seen and assured Ed that if the child could be saved this was the person to do it! He went to Esther's room to share the good news that Easy was doing fine and would make it through. The nurse gave Esther something to help her sleep and suggested she would need her strength for tomorrow!

As Ed and Roberta were leaving, Ed said, "We can put that meeting off for a while." Roberta gave her a kiss and they left the room.

Chapter Ninety-Three

The Hospital Again
June 12, 1935

Easy continued in serious condition with a low-grade fever for several days. At one point, the hospital staff feared sepsis because of the germs that might be found on a washer on the back porch of a house on Pleasant Hill. Blood-poisoning is frequently diagnosed after surgery when the white cells increase dramatically and the patient develops a high fever. It is an extremely dangerous condition, only sulfa drugs treat it. His father came to visit him for a few days and to alleviate the pressure on Esther.

Fortunately, the fever receded and the threat of sepsis passed as well. Esther took Little Easy home to the house on Pleasant Hill Road and Ez returned to his studies in Bloomington.

The hospital and doctor bills were the responsibility of Ezra and Esther. In anticipation of the inevitable, Esther and Ezra talked to Ed about a loan. There was no charge from Dr. Droulliard but instead he sent a new hundred-dollar bill to help with the hospital charges. The charge for the room and food, medications, staff services and supplies amounted to less than three hundred dollars.

Esther and Ezra wanted to pay the balance but they were living off Esther's pay and the few gigs Ez was able to pick up. She told Ed they could repay a loan at ten dollars a month if they scrimped on other expenses. There was a lot of pride involved here, so the bank agreed to work it out on that basis. Of course, Rose wanted to take up a collection at church and at Randy's Rotary Club. Ed urged them not to do that but to let matters take a natural course.

As the strength came back to Easy, he was walking around the house with his arm in a sling to protect the heavy bandages. Messages came from Dr. Droulliard from time to time urging him to take care but to perform some light exercises with his right arm. He wrote and threw a ball with his right hand but the likelihood of a full recovery of the arm was bleak.

Twice a week Esther took him to the hospital to have his bandages changed and examine the damaged area. His young body responded well and although it was tedious for many weeks and months, he achieved a full recovery.

The family and members of the church offered frequent prayers in his behalf and he was remembered every Sunday at the First Methodist Church.

Chapter Ninety-Four

The Temple Home on Pleasant Hill
Wednesday, August 14, 1935

The summer had come and almost gone when Ezra came home for a few weeks off from his graduate studies. Although the entire neighborhood had helped to care for Easy, Esther was under heavy stress. She continued her volunteer work, leading the community group and cautiously begun her volunteer role with the bank. Ed was careful not to overdo it but to keep her busy with the important work of building relationships with the folks on Pleasant Hill and a couple of ladies groups to which Roberta could wrangle an invitation to make her presentation. It was a work in progress, but Ed saw a great future for her.

It was Ezra who broached the subject after lunch, "Momma, you have carried a heavy load for the last many weeks. Why don't you take a vacation? I can look after Easy and we can get to be father and son again. We will both miss you but some time off would help you recover from the stress you have experienced."

"Why don't you mind your own business? I am just fine. Where would I go anyway?"

"I talked to Early Owens and he talked to President Eakerly at Eastern Kentucky Agricultural School and they would like for you to come down and stay in their home on the campus. Miss Rebecca is anxious to see you and to hear about Easy and your work here in the community and at the bank."

"Well, that's about the rudest thing I ever heard of. I will do no such thing. Whoever heard of me looking to be invited to spend time with them? I raised you better than that. You drop that idea right now. I do not want to hear another word about it! Where did I go wrong with you? That sounds like something your daddy would do, God bless his soul!"

Ezra did not say a word. He retreated to the room they had set up for Easy. He sat on the bench beside the bed where the boy was napping. Soon he stretched out on the floor with some children's books for a pillow. He was exhausted as well.

"Daddy, what are you doing lying on my floor? You take a nap on my cot and I will go sit on the porch. Can I have one of the books to read?"

The boy comforted his father and went to read on the front porch. It started to rain and the noise of the drops on the metal roof sounded like a heavenly song.

Later in the afternoon Ed and Roberta dropped by to see the patient. Esther fixed some tea and they sat on the porch to visit. "I'm might near out of ice. Have you seen that iceman and his broke down wagon and horse? The market wagon was by here yesterday but no ice."

Ed remarked, "It is summertime, Esther."

"All the more reason for him to come by here. The few little things I have got in my icebox will spoil without it! One of these days I want to get a Frigidaire."

Roberta noting how short Esther was in her conversation said, "Girl, you sound tired. Have you been taking care of yourself?"

"You sound like Ezra. He has been telling me I need a vacation. Where am I going to vacate to? Best I can do is go fishing over on the river. Nothing bites now; it's too hot."

Roberta looked at Ed and he nodded his head.

"Esther, Ed and I did not take a honeymoon and we are thinking of going to Lake Geneva for a few days. We want you to go with us. Randy said the bank would pay your expenses and we have room in the car."

Flattered but a little uncomfortable with the proposal, Esther asked, "Why is Randy going to pay my expenses? I am not a bank employee. I just volunteer to try to raise the quality of life for the folks on Pleasant Hill. They need to get in the habit of saving and owning a bank account. I hope to help the bank but it may be slow."

"Never mind all that. We really want you to join us!"

Still suspicious, Esther asked, "Have you been talking to that meddling son of mine?"

"What about? He is playing at the country club for a party the bank is giving and we have talked about that."

"I never heard of nobody going on a honeymoon with a new bride and groom. Ya'll go on I'll be okay."

"We'll pick you up around 10 Friday morning. I will bring you a bathing suit. We'll have a grand time."

With that, Ed and Roberta left the house and drove off. Esther was in tears.

Chapter Ninety-Five

Wednesday August 21, 1935
Esther and the Honeymooners

They came up Pleasant Hill Road about 4:00 in the afternoon. There was an overhead banner at the entry:

"Welcome Home Esther and the Honeymooners!

Your Friends at the First Bank and Trust Company and

Your Pleasant Hill Neighbors."

Easy had been sitting on the porch of the house on the corner to alert the neighbors. When they turned into the road, he rang a big dinner bell situated on a post in the yard. They began to ring cowbells, honk car horns and even a left-over firecracker was heard. It was a grand occasion, fitting for the neighborhood association president and her companions. Esther broke into tears again at the sight. Ezra came hustling out to get her luggage; he and Easy escorted her to the front porch where she waved to her friends and collapsed into a rocker. She was overcome with emotion at the unexpected reception.

When Ed and Roberta came to the porch she said, "Somebody's been up to something." Roberta just grinned and Ed lit up like a crystal chandelier. They were slightly tanned and Esther looked more fit than ever before. It had been a long haul for her: her daughter-in-law miscarried and died in childbirth; her grandchild had been kidnapped; her husband died suddenly of a stroke; she then moved from a place she loved and children she loved and taught to live in a hovel compared to the campus home she enjoyed for so many years; her son left her in charge of his son while he pursued the dream of a higher degree; and her only grandchild was in recovery from a horrible accident.

In retrospect she had every right to have accumulated enough stress to kill a mule. The trip to Lake Geneva was a gift from Heaven. She could not express her appreciation to Ed and Roberta adequately so she fell into an emotional lump. Ezra helped her into the house where she sat in the only comfortable chair in the place. Ed and Roberta followed along with Easy. The neighbors relaxed on the front porch and some brought wooden folding chairs to sit in. The men had chosen a shady spot and made a table from sawhorses and planks salvaged from the recent improvements on the street. The ladies began to appear with dozens of potluck dishes, pies, cakes and fried chicken. Randy and Rose drove up with an ice cream freezer ready for grinding, rock salt and fresh ice.

After a while, Esther dried her tears, and they persuaded her to come out and greet her neighbors and friends. Ed and Ezra brought out the comfortable chair and put it in another shady spot. Esther Temple was queen for another day.

Chapter Ninety-Six

Plowing New Ground
Monday, August 26, 1935

Ed drove over to Esther's house to line up the meeting they cancelled in June. She was stringing beans on the front porch.

"Come on in Ed. I am just getting supper ready for Easy and me. Why don't you and Roberta drop by this evening?"

"Sounds good but Roberta has to work late tonight. Can we get a rain check?"

"Of course. What's on your mind?"

"Esther, remember in June that we talked about holding a meeting at the new Community Room next to the bank. How do you feel about having it this week?"

"Our interest is as great as ever to do it."

"What day? how many folks?"

"All my neighbors would be about 35 or 40. However, let me remind you what we would like to do. We would like to have a meeting of our association and then have a reception honoring the Vice-Mayor and the County Judge. We will bring the snacks. Could you help us with the coffee and cold drinks?"

"We will stick to the original plan. We will furnish all the refreshments. Let me check on their meeting dates and get back to you."

Esther sent word up and down the road of the upcoming event. She asked some of them to come by her house this evening to talk about the issues to discuss with the politicians.

About an hour later, Ed was back: "How about Thursday the twenty-ninth? Both the County Executive and Madame Vice Mayor say that will work for them. We want to be sure she is still in the frame of mind to meet with you and your neighbors. You invite your folks and I'll get the politicians and some other city leaders."

Back at the bank, he told Roberta that the date was okay with Esther. "She will get the neighbors there."

"Our list will need to be short but heavy duty. If you make the calls to our list, I'll check with Randy and Rose."

Ed set out to list the heavy-hitters and opinion makers in town. He started with the radio station and the daily paper, the merchants association, a few preachers, some folks from the college, the city aldermen and the county magistrates. Deep down in his heart he hoped some of the aldermen and very conservative rural officials would pass. Ed knew that if one is invited all must be.

He went to his office and began the task of developing the list with names, addresses and phone numbers. It occurred to him that most of the phone calls would be made to folks with party line phones. This was not the first meeting held in their new community room but it was special. The bank was plowing new ground. Knowing the negative impact such an overture to this segment of potential customers could have on many of their current customers he had second thoughts. He must cut the list to only those who would keep the event to themselves. They would drop by to see the neighbors personally. (That meant only about 8 or 10 close friends of the bank and the top city and county leaders in addition to the County Judge and the Vice Mayor.) Roberta agreed. Randy would call most of them. Rose would pitch in with the details. A larger function could wait.

Chapter Ninety-Seven

The Queen Mother and the Politicians
Monday, August 29, 1935

The neighbors began to gather about four-thirty in the afternoon. Esther took two loads of ladies over in the big Peerless that had belonged to President Eakerly. Some of the men walked from work and some hitched a ride into the center of town on the now-empty market wagon and ice wagon. Some of those who worked in the public received permission to leave an hour or so early and arrived a little before five.

Esther called the meeting to order for a little business at five. She introduced Roberta Cummins Negley who welcomed the group and encouraged them to visit the bank for assistance anytime.

"Savings and checking accounts are a modern and convenient way to handle money. Our bank is as secure as any in Indiana, more than most. Your business is important to us and we need you just as much you need us! The ladies here today are especially important to us as you can see by the bank leadership present here today. Do not be surprised to see one of your own soon to be elected as an officer. You can guess who that will be!"

With that, the ladies gasped and then began to applaud. It was hard to tell whether the applause was for Roberta, the bank, or Esther Temple.

Esther was completely taken off-guard. When she regained her composure, she continued the agenda without comment.

The next order was to select a secretary-treasurer. No one volunteered so Esther asked if Ladye Frances Hayes would serve. With the expected reluctance, she agreed to do so.

The city and county officials began to slip in so Esther adjourned the meeting without further business. "We will meet again soon so let me know of your concerns and we can discuss them at that time."

She asked Roberta if they could continue to meet in this room until the church had been rebuilt.

"We will be honored to host you here whenever you wish. The room is also available by reservation for other social and community meetings."

Ed had come in the back door and breathed a sigh of relief that the secret plan came about as envisioned. No doubt, Roberta was correct with this idea. Randy and Rose accompanied him with smiles a mile wide and took a seat along the side.

It was indeed a new day for Fort Anthony and the First Bank and Trust!

The End

Printed in the United States
133355LV00003B/16/P